Dust
of
Power

AN ADVENTURE OF HERMAN AND HIS PALS

JAY ANDRUS

PAGE PUBLISHING, INC.
New York, NY

First originally published by Page Publishing, Inc. 2014

ISBN 978-1-63417-498-5 (pbk)
ISBN 978-1-63417-499-2 (digital)

Printed in the United States of America

For my four daughters, grandchildren, and nieces and nephews, who have known Herman and his Pals for many years.

As the group arrived outside the clearing, Herman and his pals beheld a scene seldom witnessed by faeries, and never before by anyone but the inhabitants of the faerie kingdom. The group came to a halt at what the pals assumed was the entrance to the clearing. The king whispered to Herman, "Please wait here. The queen has been busy. I know now what she is doing. Other faeries will join you here. The rest of us must go into the clearing to prepare for your entrance."

The pals were completely flustered. "I think some kind of council has been convened, and we're not supposed to be here," whispered Goossey.

PROLOGUE

Herman and his pals are four boys. They are ten to twelve years old, although their actual age isn't really that important. Herman is sort of the leader, not because he is the oldest or the biggest; he is just the leader. Herman and his pals are not a gang. They are just four good friends enjoying their youth.

It is almost a proven fact that all groups of boys have nicknames for each other. This is very personal and people outside the group don't understand where the names come from, so they might think them silly. But Herman and his pals like their nicknames.

Herman's nickname is Herman the German. Why? One might ask. Herman has a good reason for his nickname, just as do all of his pals. His nickname comes from the fact that his grandparents came from Germany, and it rhymes—Herman the German. He is tall and broad in the shoulders, yet lean and somewhat muscular for a boy his age. He has blond wavy hair, and his distinct facial features with a square jaw and high cheekbones combined with a clear commanding voice and piercing blue eyes make him a natural leader. He is the largest of the pals, but never takes advantage of it. Herman is very proud of his heritage. Germany is a marvelous country with lots of mountains and forests.

The next pal's nickname is Cheesey the Wheezy. Cheesey is almost as tall as Herman, but with light brown, curly hair, and a comfortable round face and hazel eyes. He is the most soft-spoken of the pals, with a slight hoarse quality to his voice, which can be suddenly very strong if he wants to be heard. He is not as obviously muscular as Herman and Moussey, but one must not be fooled by his wiry frame. He is strong and quick. His pals call him Cheesey for short. The origin of his name is not complicated. He loves cheese, and once, when he was much younger, he had a bad cold that caused him to make very weird sounds when he breathed. The sound is called wheezing, thus Cheesey the Wheezy.

The next pal's nickname is Moussey the Loussey. This may not seem like a very complimentary nickname, but he is called Moussey for short. Moussey is built much like Herman and is just as tall. He has dark brown wavy hair and a smile that makes everyone immediately his friend. One time when he was much younger, Moussey was playing in his back yard with his pals. These boys have been friends for a long time. He saw a mouse in the garden and thought it was cute. So he decided to catch it and keep it for a pet. It never became his pet, but he did get some bugs from it called lice, not a very pleasant story. Moussey's parents had to have him deloused, and his pals never forgot the incident. Pals can call someone things that others would not be allowed to call them because they are good friends. Thus, Moussey the Loussey.

The last pal in the group has a very interesting nickname, Goossey the Lucy. Goossey is shorter than the other three pals and has curly black hair. He isn't fat, but because he is not as tall as the other three, he might appear more round in appearance than his three tall, lean buddies. He has dark brown eyes and a happy disposition. When Goossey was much younger, he had a pet goose. He and the goose were very good friends, which is somewhat unusual; geese are very big birds, and some can be quite mean. But this goose was a very devoted pet, and it followed Goossey everywhere. The goose's name was Lucy. Lucy finally got very old and died, but the nickname stayed. Goossey likes the nickname because it reminds him of his very good friend, Lucy the goose.

Through all of their adventures, Herman and his pals will be called by their nicknames.

Herman and his pals live in the Midwest of the United States. This part of the United States has many forests. Not far from the homes of Herman and his pals is a deep, dark, thick forest. The pals often play around this forest. They have played around it all their lives, but they never have gone very far into it. They are not afraid; their parents simply taught them to be cautious. One day, during one of their many camping trips, they were playing 500, and Goossey hit the ball too hard and it went too far. The adventure begins.

CHAPTER ONE

THE PALS' FOREST

"Oh great, Goossey!" Herman exclaimed. "You hit it into the forest. How are we ever going to find it?"

"We'll just have to go home and get another ball," chimed in Moussey.

But Cheesey reminded them, "You know this was our last ball. Our parents told us we can't buy another one until we find the other ten we lost in the forest."

"Okay," asserted Goossey, "we'll just have to go in and look for it."

"Right!" yelled Moussey as he entered the forest. "We might as well get started."

"But how deep will we have to go?" asked Cheesey.

"As deep as it takes!" declared Herman as he followed Moussey into the forest.

Cheesey and Goossey looked at each other and said together, "Well, let's get it over with."

So the pals entered the forest. Now they had played for years around the outside of the forest and had gone a little ways into it, but they knew that the ball had gone quite deep into the forest. They would have to go farther than they had ever gone before.

"Okay, guys," directed Herman, asserting himself as the leader of the group. "Let's stay together. We can spread out but always be where the next guy can see you."

"Good idea," agreed Cheesey.

As the pals entered the forest, they forgot about the ball, the real reason for going in. They simply used the ball as an excuse to do what they had always wanted to do, really explore the forest. As they got deeper into the forest, they realized more and more how beautiful it was, more beautiful than they had ever imagined. Suddenly Goossey had an important thought.

"We better figure a way to mark the trail or we'll never find our way out of this place! Anybody got an idea how we do it?"

"We could break off twigs and limbs," Cheesey suggested.

"I don't think we would be able to find them later," said Herman doubtfully.

"I have an idea. It's late and we will not get too far into the forest before dark, and I don't want to be in there after dark until I know where we are going and how to get out," complained Goossey.

Herman supported him. "Goossey's right. Let's go home and figure a way to mark the trail and get an early start in the morning."

"Then our moms can replenish our food supply," added Moussey.

So they went home and asked their parents about ideas for marking trails. The dads suggested notching the trees with knives, but the pals didn't want to hurt the trees.

"It won't hurt the trees," said Herman's father. "You're not going to use an axe."

Herman wanted to use another method if they could find it.

Just then the telephone rang. It was Cheesey. "My mom has a great idea. She has some pink ribbon that we can tie to trees and bushes. If none of the other guys find out, who cares if we use bright pink ribbon. It would work!"

Herman called the other pals to Cheesey's house for a planning session.

"It would be easy to see," said Goossey. "We could tie the pieces at intervals close enough to be able to see the next one from where the last one is tied."

"Then we wouldn't have to look too hard for each mark," added Moussey.

"Okay then. Are we agreed? We use Cheesey's mom's bright pink . . . does it have to be pink ribbon?" asked Herman. The other pals nodded.

"Okay, pink it is. But don't tell anyone about this. We will never live it down. Pink ribbon. Girls!"

All agreed with Herman. "Girls are not going into the forest with us tomorrow. Now let's get on with the plans," directed Goossey.

The pals planned to leave very early. Their parents were not really surprised as the pals often went hiking and camping and discovering.

So early the next morning, they stood outside of the forest, ready to embark on the greatest adventure of their entire lives.

"Well, let's get started," murmured Goossey quietly. "We've got food and have told our parents that we will be gone for a few days camping, so what are we waiting for?"

Into the forest they went. They didn't have to leave ribbons immediately because they knew the outskirts of the forest very well. They knew the boundaries of the "known areas." When they got beyond these boundaries, they would start the ribbons.

The sky was blue and cloudless. The sunbeams filtered through the leaves giving an almost enchanted feeling to the forest, making it deep green and quiet.

"This is beautiful," remarked Cheesey.

They walked single file, with Herman in the lead.

As they got deeper into the forest, the sun did not penetrate the thick leaves enough to let in as much light as the pals would have liked. The forest was not dark, however, just deep green and still very quiet.

The pals had a feeling of contentment and peace, not fear. This was a friendly forest. They felt strangely secure, even though they didn't know where they were going, or how far they would have to go to get to the other side.

"You know," said Moussey, "I should be scared or something, but I really feel at home here. Why didn't we come this far before?"

"We really have been missing something," added Goossey.

"We are the first to do this: I'm sure of it," said Herman. "This is brand-new territory. No one has ever been this deep in the forest before."

"What a first!" said Goossey quietly. Then he realized something. "Oh no! The beauty of the forest has made us forget to tie the ribbons!"

They turned around and the forest seemed to close in around them. Not in a frightening way, but like a warm blanket of leaves, shrubs, flowers, and trees. But the pals were a little worried. They could see a little where they had come; the underbrush was trampled down somewhat.

"Do we go back?" asked Cheesey.

"Which way?" asked Moussey.

"The way we came. It's easy to see the way we came," Herman replied.

So they started back but found that the underbrush had bounced back very quickly when they had gone but a short distance.

"This is a very young and strong forest," said Goossey.

"I think it is a very old forest," contradicted Cheesey. "It is old and strong."

"But not frightening!" exclaimed Herman. "If we can't go back, then let's go on. We have to get to the other side sometime. We have four days."

"Herm's right," said Moussey with enthusiasm.

"Let's give it a shot!" added Cheesey. "It can't be that far to the other side."

The others looked at each other in disbelief.

"What a dumb statement!" said Herman. "We've never been all the way around this forest. We have no idea how far it is. It could be miles."

"Herm is right!" Moussey continued. "If we are not going back, then let's go to the right or left and then we'll get to the side of the forest instead of going all the way through it."

The others looked at each other in disbelief.

"If the forest is round, it will be just as far to the right or left as it is to find the other side," said Goossey. "Any way could be the longest way out."

"Only if we are in the middle of the forest," speculated Herman. "I don't think we have walked far enough to get to the middle yet."

"Then let's walk to the middle and then turn to the left or right," Cheesey continued.

The others looked at each other in disbelief.

"How will we know when we are at the middle, oh wise one of the earth?" asked Goossey.

"We won't know," said Herman. "But are we on an adventure or not? Let's start hanging ribbon from here on and then we can at least get back to here."

"Then we could try and go on from here. This is the closest to the edge that we know!" cried Moussey. "What have we got to lose?"

"Only our lives," murmured Cheesey. The pals had to admit that they were just a little bit scared. They couldn't see the sun, only the rays that filtered through the thick cover of the forest, so they couldn't get a direction.

"I think we'd better go back. It is the surest way, if there is one," said Goossey.

They all agreed. Just as they turned to try and retrace their steps, a bright flash filled the forest in the direction they were trying to go.

"What was that?" exclaimed Herman.

"Maybe it was lightning," said Moussey.

"Then where is the thunder?" quietly asked Cheesey.

"I think we should continue and investigate," asserted Herman, trying to sound courageous.

They took one step and another bright flash, brighter than the first, filled their eyes with brilliant pain.

"I think we shouldn't go that way," Goossey asserted.

Herman got an idea. "Let's try the right." A flash met their attempt.

"How about the left?" asked Moussey, catching on to what Herman was doing. Before they ever took a step, another flash met their eyes, not as bright as the previous ones.

"Guys, I don't know what is going on, but I think the way is forward," said Goossey. So forward they went.

CHAPTER TWO

New Friends

As they went forward, the forest became denser, and the greens got deeper, and the sun's rays filtering through the canopy produced little flickerings of light on the bushes and flowers. After a while, the pals noticed that the flickering was not only the sun's rays.

"Do you see what I see?" asked Moussey.

"Yes," replied Herman, "but I'm not sure I want to admit it! This is weird!"

The extra flashes seemed to the pals like the fireflies that they loved to watch and even catch and put in jars and watch them light up like a lantern.

"This can't be the sun's rays being filtered through the leaves," said Goossey. "This is more like little points of light."

"Like a flash bulb," added Moussey.

The pals noticed that the flicks of light were leading them toward a group of very large trees with extremely dense leaves. They looked like they would shut out all light if someone were in the middle of them. Yet, they were being led toward that grove of trees. As they got closer to the grove, the flicks of light seemed to draw together.

"You know," said Cheesey, "if these flicks of light happened all at once, they could make a bright flash."

"Maybe that's where the bright flashes came from," said Goossey.

"I think we are about to find out," said Herman as he saw the huge trees suddenly lean apart, creating a spectacular arched entrance into the grove.

As they entered, the "gate" closed behind them, the only sound being the rustling of the leaves coming together.

They found themselves in a grove of trees that rose hundreds of feet above them. The trunks were of the most delicate light brown color. The ground was covered with a soft green grass, with beautiful multicolored flowers growing in it.

"I've never felt anything so soft in my life!" exclaimed Moussey. "This grass is the most beautiful green I have ever seen!"

"I want to take my shoes off and feel it!" whispered Goossey.

"And look at the flowers!" exclaimed Cheesey.

There were not only flowers in the carpet of grass, but all around it, making a kind of circle along with the trees of the grove. The trees were very thick and dense where the "circle" ended, making it impossible to leave the grove.

"You know," said Herman, "I know I should be scared, but this place is so peaceful and beautiful, I could stay here forever."

"Yeah, I agree," said Cheesey, "but let's get serious. Have you ever seen trees like this before?"

"Now that you ask, no!" said Goossey.

"Come on, guys, have you seen all the trees in the world?" demanded Herman.

"No," responded Moussey, "but this bark is almost as soft as the grass. Feel it!"

"But it is also very hard. I can't break it with my knife!" exclaimed Herman.

"What are you doing trying to stick your knife into that tree!" cried Cheesey.

"I'm not going to cut it!" responded Herman, a little put out that Cheesey would think he could try to hurt it.

"Sorry, I just got carried away with the feel of the bark."

"Well, what do we do now?" quietly asked Goossey.

"We wait!" answered his pal, Herman.

So the pals sat down in the middle of the most beautiful place they had ever seen—and waited.

"Let's eat something!" said Cheesey, wanting to try the new cheese his mother had put on his sandwich.

"Why not?" the others said in unison. So they ate some lunch.

After eating, they decided to try and find their way out of the grove. When they tried to leave, the undergrowth, although very beautiful and green, seemed to pull together and form a barrier wherever they tried to get out.

"Guess we're not supposed to leave," said Moussey.

Time passed. Still nothing more happened. No more flicks of light, no more movement of the trees—nothing.

Herman started to notice it was getting dark. "The sun is going down, guys."

"Yeah, I noticed that too," said Cheesey, a little nervously.

"Somehow I feel very protected though," said Moussey, "as if I were being watched over, or something."

"Or something," added Goossey.

"Well, the carpet is very soft. Let's get some sleep," said Herman. "There sure isn't anything else to do."

They lay down, but didn't go to sleep; they were too excited to shut their eyes.

"I wish my bed at home were this soft," said Moussey.

The sun went down. The pals knew that it had set because the rays through the leaves were more dim. But as the sun's rays got dimmer, the grove stayed light.

"This is weird, man," said Goossey.

"There is light coming from up in the trees!" cried Moussey.

19

"Yeah, a soft glow. I wonder what is going on," said Herman.

"Say, do you guys believe in little people?" asked Moussey.

"You mean like leprechauns and faeries and pixies and stuff like that?" asked Cheesey.

"Yeah, and stuff like that."

"You've got to admit that this is not something we see every day. Right, guys?" asked Herman. "This glow that is lighting this grove is not the sun."

"And it's not the moon either," said Goossey. "The moonlight couldn't get through those trees."

The others looked at each other in disbelief.

"Moonlight isn't bright yellow gold like this either," they all said together.

"You know," cried Cheesey, "we are sitting here in this beautiful place talking about the sun and moon and this strange light source as if it is common knowledge. Let's get serious. This isn't normal and it's time we found out what is going on."

"And just what do you propose doing?" asked Goossey, not very politely. "Asking the little people who are causing this to happen to reveal themselves?"

"Boy, are you something else," added Herman.

"Wait a minute. Yes! Let's ask if it's little people doing this. What have we got to lose?" exclaimed Cheesey.

"You're the one who came up with the idea, Moussey. You ask them," directed Goossey.

"Why me? I don't know how to talk to little people. One of you do it?"

"Let's all do it!" cried Cheesey.

What followed was one of the strangest sights one would ever see, these four pals walking around the edge of the grove, or crawling on their knees, saying, "Hello, little people. Where are you? Would you like to come out and play? Are you here?" and other such ridiculous things, things that would be ridiculous under normal circumstances. But these were not normal circumstances.

Then the most marvelous thing happened. Little spots of light started to descend from the golden canopy of light above the pals.

These spots became brighter and brighter until they landed on the grass, the bushes, the leaves of small trees and flowers. As they came to rest, the pals noticed that they were, to their total surprise and astonishment—very tiny people.

They were about twelve inches high, both men and women. But to Herman and his pals, they looked more like tiny children. The men, because that is what they were, were dressed in pants and shirts of many shades of green, brown, blue, and yellow. Their shoes were pointed and made of what seemed to be soft leather of matching colors. They wore little pointed hats. The women were dressed in little skirts and blouses and tights in the same soft, natural hues. They also had little pointed shoes, but no hats. The most amazing thing about all of this was the little pair of wings on each of their backs. The pals thought at first that they used the wings to fly, but the wings didn't move when the little people moved from place to place. These little people were all around the pals. They counted ten of them. Then all of a sudden, a bright golden glow came down from higher in the grove. The pals saw that the glow was caused by several little people dressed like the others, and in the middle were two little people dressed like the others only all in gold, and they had tiny crowns on their heads. They descended until they were at eye level with the pals, landing lightly on the leaves of a very large, beautiful shrub.

"Did you see the bush get flowers just as those two with the crowns landed on it?" asked Herman.

"Yeah," said Cheesey. "There were no flowers until they landed on it."

"These really are little people?" exclaimed Goossey.

The others looked at each other in disbelief.

"No, they are the giants of the forest," said Moussey, a little sarcastically.

"Shush, guys!" directed Herman. "I think this must be the king and queen of the little people. Show a little respect."

The pals waited for the king and queen to speak.

The queen, although very tiny, was one of the most beautiful women that they had ever seen, and the king was also very handsome. Even though they were tiny, they commanded respect and adoration.

The other little people gathered about the king and queen, some of them above them, maintaining the glow in the grove, and some sitting on the grass, others on the shrubs and leaves of the trees.

The king and queen did not speak. They just continued to look at the pals, as if they were appraising their strengths and weaknesses.

Herman finally spoke. "Your Majesties, I assume you are majesties, we are . . ."

"We know who you are," said the king in a very strong, not low, but not too high voice, immediately commanding respect. "We've been watching you for a very long time."

The pals looked at each other in surprise and disbelief. "How long have you watched us?" respectfully asked Cheesey.

Suddenly all of the balls lost during the many games of 500 came showering on them from above.

"For two years," said the queen. Her voice fell on their ears with such softness that they wondered if she had spoken, but there was strength in her voice that left no doubt that she had spoken. "From the time that you started playing more and more in our wood, we have wondered if you would ever come this far into the forest."

"We didn't mean to do anything wrong," explained Goossey in a very pitiful voice. "We were just exploring."

"You are very brave explorers," said the king. "You are also very creative in your play and seem to plan very carefully what you want to do."

Moussey wanted very badly to ask an important question. So he finally did. "You said this is your wood. How long have you lived here? These trees are very big, bigger than any we have ever seen."

"And this place is so beautiful," added Herman, gaining a little courage from his pals. "How do you make the light when there is no sun?"

"And where does this beautiful grass come from?" asked Goossey.

"And the beautiful flowers?" chimed in Moussey.

"And how did that plant make flowers when you landed on it?" quickly asked Herman, gaining even more courage from the questions of his pals.

"And how do you keep from falling on the ground? You seem to be able to stand in the air. Do you control gravity?" asked Moussey.

All of the above questions were asked in a very short time and all at once.

The queen laughed. The sound was so pleasant, the pals were suddenly silent.

"You boys are just delightful," she said. "You have no fear, just marvelous curiosity and desire to find out what is going on and why."

"We didn't offend you, did we?" asked Cheesey. "We don't know you at all, but we wouldn't want to do something to hurt or offend you in any way."

"That's right," added the rest of the pals all at once.

"No, you haven't done anything but confirm all we have discovered and thought while we observed you," said the king. "This is not really our home forest. It is our home in your country."

"We come from very far away, but this forest is a refuge for us when we want to relax and see new things," said the queen. "We planted these trees here many years ago. You are the first big people ever to see them."

"But why us and not our parents?" asked Goossey.

"Because your parents don't come to the forest, and they would not accept us as easily as you do," answered the king. "They would have a hard time believing their eyes. You don't even question our existence."

"Yes," joined the queen, "the fact that we really exist is a great joy to you."

"But why did you wait until now to talk to us?" asked Herman. "You led us deep in the forest."

"Yeah," said Moussey, "we might have come this far, but you made sure we did."

"And guiding us to this grove is no coincidence!" cried Cheesey, gaining more and more courage.

"You are right," said the queen. "We needed to make contact with you this time. We have need of you and your friendship, and hopefully your help."

"We have watched you play your games. You think them out very carefully," said the king. "You are very strong boys, quite big for your ages."

"And you are courageous and not afraid to try something new," added the queen. She looked at her husband the king, with an anxious look in her eyes, almost fear.

"Hey, what is going on?" asked Goossey. "You seem to be almost afraid."

The other little people seemed to draw near. "We need someone who believes in us, and who accepts us, to help us!" cried the king, jumping to Herman's knee, almost scaring him to death.

Herman knew that the king must need his help very badly to approach him in this manner. "We are in very great danger in our home forest. We cannot take care of our problem alone. We need some big people that we can trust to help us!"

The king flitted back to the shrub. "I'm sorry if I frightened you," he added quietly, looking first to Herman and then to each of the other pals.

"Will you help us?" implored the queen.

"Yes, will you help us?" cried the others together as a chorus.

"Tell us what you need us to do," said Herman, looking at each of the pals for approval.

"Yes! Tell us what we can do!" cried the other pals.

The king looked at the queen, and then at all of the other little people, and then at Herman and his pals, and began to speak.

CHAPTER THREE

THE EXPLANATION

"This wood is a very small copy of our home forest. Our whole forest is like this one, near a place you call Germany. The king looked at his wife, the queen, and continued. "Our home forest is very wide and long. Its vastness helps protect us from the big people and others who would want to control it if they knew of the great powers it contains. We have lived there for many years and no one has ever found us or really knows of our existence, unless we want them to. Many, many years ago we talked to big people whom we thought could be trusted and be our true friends and not tell anyone about us. We have not talked to any big people since. This way we have lived in our forest without anyone knowing about us—except . . ." The king became very quiet and looked very afraid. He stopped talking like he couldn't say any more.

The queen tenderly put her arm about her husband and continued, "There are many little people in the world. They are all our friends, but we don't want to cause them any harm, so we came looking for someone else to help us. There are others who also live near our forest. We discovered them long ago. They did not bother us at first. Recently they have become curious about our beautiful forest and they come to investigate. We fear they are very greedy, and we have what you would call, great wealth—what you call jewels, gold, and silver, only far more beautiful and pure than anything you have ever seen. Our power protects our forest so the big people won't cut it down or destroy it in any way. But 'they' came a long time ago. They are strangers to our ways and live in the mountains near our forest. We think they live in caves and love the dark, not the light, especially our kind of light!" She stopped. Her voice had changed; it was frightening and loud, not as sweet at it had been. The pals could see that she was afraid. They had never seen anyone so frightened.

After a long silence Moussey whispered, "Who are—they?"

The queen looked at her husband for support and strength. She knew what had to be said. But he gently put up his hand to stop her. "I should be the one to tell them, my dear one." The king looked at the others around and above him. The other faeries seemed to hunch down as if they were trying to hide from what he was going to say. The pals noticed that their light was not as bright as it had been.

"You must tell us who 'they' are," said Herman, very respectfully and quietly, as he could see the king did not want to say what he had to say.

"If you want our help, we must know what we are going to have to do," said Cheesey.

"THE GOBLINS!" cried the king. His voice was not his own commanding, firm kingly voice. As he said the words, his voice became harsh, almost a scream, but a scream of sadness and terror. When he said the words, the light in the glade went out. The pals were left in complete darkness. They felt the oppression of the words and the fear of the faeries as they had listened to the words.

The pals sat quietly, feeling the fear of the king and queen and their people around them. The fear was almost more than the pals could stand. Finally Goossey cried out in a loud voice, "Please don't leave us in the dark! Come back with your light!"

They then noticed a gentle light start to grow in the middle of the glade, behind them. As they turned, it grew and grew until it was almost too bright for them to look at. They had to shade their eyes. It was the faerie queen in all her glory, well, not quite all her glory; it would have been too much for them without the proper protection. Then a glow started at her side; it was her husband, the king. As his light grew, she dimmed her light, but the two together filled the whole glen with light. Shading their eyes, the pals felt something fall on them, gentle and warm, like a quiet rain, yet dry. Glancing at their hands and arms and clothing, they saw that they were covered in what they thought was pure gold dust, with little glittering specks of silver. The king and queen became even brighter, but the pals could look on them without squinting or shading their eyes. People, perhaps even their parents, outside the forest that looked toward the forest that night would have thought they were seeing the northern lights. The glow of the king and queen of the faeries in all their glory was not a light that could be hidden by any amount of forest. The light shot high in the sky, a shaft of golden light that reached so high it became a golden point of light. If anyone had been able to follow it, they would have seen it go far out into space.

Then suddenly the glen was dark again, but only for the blink of an eye. A gentle glow began to come from where the pals had seen the king and queen in all their glory, but this time it was the other faeries making the glow. The king spoke, quietly and firmly, again the kingly voice they had heard the first time he spoke. "I thank my dear wife for showing courage in this great time of fear and need."

CHAPTER FOUR

THE DUST

Herman and his pals were quite possibly the only humans ever to see such a display of the power from these small, gentle beings. Cheesey was the first to speak. "Your Majesties, we really don't know what to say or do. We are willing to help, but surely you don't need us with such great power as you have just demonstrated."

The king gently placed his tiny hand on Cheesey's knee. "We cannot maintain a display of power like you just witnessed for a very long time. It takes too much out of us. We cannot fight in this manner for very long. The light would no doubt be blinding to the goblins, but we don't know if it would be permanent. If it weren't permanent, then they would just learn to cover their eyes and then come after us with even more energy and determination. No, we have to find other ways of fighting them. Maybe a show of power would be useful at the end of a battle just to frighten them, but it would be necessary to have already won the war."

"And my young friends," said the queen, "this is a war. It is a war for our very lives and existence. Let us tell you what we want in more detail."

She looked up above her head. One of the faeries glided down and lightly landed on a leaf in front of the pals. "My name is Andron, and I am head of our army, which is kind of silly; we have never had an army; we have never needed one. Andron's shirt was green like the leaves of the forest and his pants were light brown; his coat yellow, his hat blue as were his shoes. "I have convinced the king and queen that you," he was looking at all of the pals, "would be better leaders of the army than I would. We have watched you play war and battles here in the forest. Your people have always been at war; you know more about it."

"You are right, Andron. Unfortunately, we do know about war. But we have never actually been in a war. We only play at it," added Moussey.

"This war," said the king, "is not like one you would fight in your world. We feel you could adapt yourselves to our war and use ideas that you have learned from your people. The goblins would not know any-thing about your world. They don't know the methods you would use."

"We cannot go to anyone else in your world for help," said Andron. "You are our only hope."

"We don't know anyone else we can trust!" chimed in one of the other faeries sitting near the king. Herman and his pals were amazed that the others would speak.

"Yes, we can all talk!" exclaimed another, her tiny hands on her hips in impatience. She was sitting on a leaf above the queen. "My name is Shandra," said the very beautiful girl faerie.

"I'm sorry we looked so surprised," said Herman. "We really aren't used to any of you. It will take us some time."

"You have to be patient with our oldest daughter," said the queen. "She is very proud of our people and doesn't always think before she speaks." The queen shot a quick, reproving glance at her impatient daughter.

"I'm sorry," Shandra said, apologizing. "We aren't used to talking to you either." Moussey had never seen a girl so beautiful in all his life. She was dressed in a soft yellow that perfectly matched her golden hair, which was short and cut close to her head, kind of like a boy's haircut.

"Our oldest thinks she should have been a prince instead of a princess. She has the courage of any one of the male faeries," explained the king. "She will be an important part of the army you will train and lead." The king almost ended this last sentence with a question. The faeries were still not sure Herman and his pals would help them, even though they had said they would. A real war would not be just a game.

"When do we get on with this war!" exclaimed Goossey. "If the war is in your home forest, then we need to get there. How do we do it?"

The other three pals were glad that one of them had finally said something to make a commitment. They all wanted to do it, but didn't know quite how to say it. "Yes, let's get there and get on with solving the goblin problem in your home forest," said Herman.

"But how do we get there?" asked Cheesey.

The other faeries giggled as Shandra, with a mischievous twinkle in her eyes, said, "We have our ways."

"Shandra," corrected the queen. "Be polite."

"With your permission, sire," said Andron, bowing low to the king.

"Let's get on with it," said the king.

All of the faeries, except the king and queen, softly glided to a point exactly above the pals' heads. The pals were amazed that they didn't ever really see or hear any movement of their wings.

As the pals looked at the faeries above their heads, the faeries turned over on their backs, still suspended in the air, straightened their legs out, as if they were lying in bed on their backs, and moved their wings. As the faeries did this movement with their wings, the pals saw something coming down on them. It looked like very delicate particles of dust, only with a light source of its own, sometimes silver, and sometimes gold, making it twinkle like a million tiny stars. As the "dust" settled upon the pals, they felt like they were enveloped in a light warm blanket. Then, to their delightful surprise, they felt themselves start to rise into the air.

The queen must have seen some fear and wonder in their eyes because she made an explanation to them of what was happening. "The faerie dust that is falling on you will give you the ability to fly extremely fast without feeling the rush of the air around you, so you can continue to breath, like the protective envelope that your airplanes have around them, only you will go much faster."

"How do you make the dust?" asked Cheesey.

She answered with a gentle smile. "We produce it in our wings, when we want to."

"Will they have enough for us to get to your forest?" asked Herman, with a little fear in his voice. "I don't want to have it run out in the middle of the Atlantic."

"We think there will be no problem," said the queen. "We will be at your sides to replenish the dust if necessary. You may even have it after you return home. You must be careful with the dust on you. If you think of flying, you will fly."

"That could be awkward," said Goossey.

"You will learn to control the ability long before you return home," reassured the queen. "It's the power of the thought, not just thinking about it. You really have to want to go from one place to another for the dust to work."

The dust suddenly stopped falling. "You'll be just fine," said Shandra.

"But we started to rise without thinking about flying. We didn't know what the dust was going to do!" said Moussey. "Does the dust have a mind of its own?"

This whole conversation was taking place in the air, about ten feet above the ground. "When nonfaeries first get the dust, it makes them rise, just by its own power. In a few moments, you will lightly descend to the ground," said Andron. "As you feel yourself descending, think that you want to stay up and see what happens."

"Do we really have time to do all of this?" asked Herman.

"If we don't, you may hurt yourselves flying into trees," said the king. "The dust will make you move faster than you can possibly imagine. If you don't learn to control its power, you may be killed!"

"Now he tells us," said Cheesey.

"Would you have said no if we had told you?" asked Shandra, a little fearful that the pals were going to change their minds.

"Heck no!" yelled Herman, who had gone about forty feet above the ground while no one was noticing, "We still would have done it. There is no way for anyone to prepare someone for this experience."

"How did you get up there?" asked Goossey.

"Just thought—go up slowly," answered Herman, as he slowly descended. "The dust responds to the slightest thought."

"You took a risk!" said Andron sternly.

"How else are we going to learn if we don't start taking the risk?" said Herman. "This risk is nothing compared to fighting goblins."

The other three pals were now rising. "Hey! This really works!" exclaimed Goossey.

The rest of the faeries descended to the ground, to give the pals the room they would need in the air.

Before long, the pals were moving up and down, side to side, diagonal, all directions, but slowly. "When do we experiment with flying speed?" asked Goossey, a little impatiently.

The king and queen looked at each other with relief and pleasure. They had not really known if the boys would be able to control, or want to control the dust. Maybe they would be afraid. "We have chosen well," said the queen, with obvious relief.

"Shandra, Andron, and the rest of the faeries will teach you," said the king. "Make sure there are no obstructions above the forest canopy," said the king to one of the faeries. "We don't want to fly into a plane or something."

The faerie seemed to disappear. "Where did she go?" asked Cheesey.

"She just demonstrated the speed at which you can travel," said the queen. "I think she was showing off a little, but it lets you know the potential of the dust."

"And the danger if you don't know what you're doing," added Moussey.

The faerie was suddenly there again. "All clear," she said, "we have all the room we need."

"What is your name?" asked Moussey.

"Orria," she answered.

"Would you take me to the top of the forest canopy so I can have some room to navigate?" asked Cheesey with a grin.

Orria, dressed in brown with long light brown hair tied in what we would call a ponytail, enhanced by twinkling brown eyes, looked at the king and queen. "Good idea," said the king. "Each of you take one of the pals under your wings," he said with a wink of an eye.

"I'll take Herman," said Shandra.

"I'll take Goossey," said Andron.

"I'll take Moussey," said a faerie all dressed in delicate green. "My name is Greena." She was very pretty, and Moussey was very happy to have *her* teach him.

"Just one question first," said Herman. "What was the dust that gave the light to the glade earlier?"

"A good question," said the queen. "That is the dust of light. We make it by rubbing our hands together. The faster we rub our hands, the brighter it becomes."

"Okay, just checking," said Herman.

"We also control it by thought," said Andron. "That's why it suddenly went out and then came back. It is kind of complicated." "We can also control its intensity by combining our thoughts," added Orria.

"Let's get going!" yelled Herman rising toward the canopy of the forest. "We can learn the powers we don't understand when we have done what needs to be done."

"Then we will be learning about everything," said Moussey to Greena, as both of them continued to rise to the top of the forest.

"You are doing very well!" exclaimed Shandra to all of the pals as they arrived at the top of the forest canopy. "You are doing all of this movement on your own, you know. We cannot control the dust of someone else."

They suddenly emerged into the star riddled sky above the forest. It was the most beautiful and exciting experience they had ever had. They could see the forest as a dark, almost black carpet under them, and the stars twinkling above them.

"I have never felt so close to the stars," murmured Cheesey, with breathless amazement in his voice.

"It is something I never get used to," said Andron.

"There is a marvelous freedom with the power of the dust," added Greena. "We have to learn how to use it, as young faeries, just like you're doing now."

"Then we are not just awkward dumb boys?" asked Goossey, encouraged by Greena's remark.

"No," said the king who, with his wife, seemed to suddenly appear beside them. "You will learn, just like we all had to." The pals noticed that the king and queen were a little brighter than the other faeries, yet all of them had a delicate glow about them.

"Hey! We have a glow too!" exclaimed an amazed Goossey.

"It's the flying dust," said Andron.

"Well, let's get on with the lessons so we can get this job done," said Herman, with an authority in his voice that surprised him.

The other pals looked at each other, then smiled, looked at Herman, grinned and said together, "Okay, boss."

"Hey, guys, I . . ."

"It's okay, Herm," said Cheesey. "You have always been the leader of the group, and someone has to be the general. You are it!"

"Right!" said the others.

The king added his approval. "You are young, but you are the one." Herman looked around at the other pals and the faeries. They were all looking at him with anticipation in their faces like, "Well, what do we do now?"

"Okay, let's get this flying process mastered, so we can get on with our mission!"

CHAPTER FIVE

FLYING

Shandra and Andron rose slightly above the rest. "We will be the lesson directors," said Andron. "Once the flying dust is on you, you merely think what you want and your body responds."

"You did it without knowing when you rose to the top of the forest," said Shandra, looking at Herman. "All you did was think and you did it."

"But you didn't know that you were doing it, so you rose kind of slowly," added Greena. She looked at Cheesey, then at Andron. Andron nodded his head. "Just think what you want, Cheesey, and it will happen."

"But you must learn to always check where you are going, or you may run into a tree or something," said Orria.

"You can be badly injured or even killed, if you are not very careful," said the king in such a serious voice that the boys knew that this flying was no joke.

"We usually learn to fly over a very long period of time," said Shandra. Looking at her parents for approval and receiving a positive nod of their heads, she continued, "But you can't take all the time we took to master flying."

"How long was that?" asked Goossey with a little fear and wonder in his voice.

"Three years, before we really start to fly at travel speed," answered Greena.

"I know it is asking a lot of you," said the king, almost with apology, "but we have no choice."

"If you want to back out and go home, we will understand," said the queen.

"Back out!" exclaimed Herman, in disbelief. "What do you say, guys? Do we back out and go home . . ."

Before he could finish his sentence, the other three pals yelled together, "NO!"

"You are flying, suspended here in the air, without fear," said Shandra, excitedly. She had already assumed that the boys would not back out, so she moved on with the flying lesson. It was obvious that she was a princess and a leader. "Did you notice that the king seemed to appear beside you, as if from nowhere? Well . . . he just thought himself there and moved almost at the speed of thought."

"For short distances, we can do that," said Orria. "It will be very helpful in battle." Orria was very young and enthusiastic. She was looking forward to the war with the goblins. It was an adventure for her.

"Wow!" said Moussey, "we almost forgot why we are doing all of this. We do have to fight a war!"

"Think of moving to a place nearby," said Andron. "One at a time at first—so you don't run into each other."

Each of the pals thought of moving to a place nearby and was amazed at the speed at which they moved, almost the instant they thought, they were there.

"Okay," said Moussey, "let's see if this really works. Someone has to try it out." Suddenly he was gone, a streak of golden light. The others, faeries and pals alike, did not move, and it was lucky they didn't for a moment later he was back.

"Where did you go?" asked Herman, a little put out.

"Home," said Moussey, as if it had been a simple walk.

"Home?" said Goossey. "I don't know how far away that is, but it's farther than the time you were gone!"

"I had to know the range of the dust with my thought," explained Moussey. "We will all have to know the range when we get into battle. It may save ours' or someone else's life."

The king looked at the queen. "We have chosen well," he said, with great relief in his voice. "Moussey is absolutely correct. You must test the range of the dust as it relates to your thoughts."

"This is very advanced training," said the queen, a bit doubtful.

"But they have to do it, so they might as well get started!" exclaimed Orria.

The next thing they knew, Herman was gone then Goossey, then Cheesey, three streaks of light trailing off in the distance. They all returned shortly after they left.

"You all went home?" asked Greena.

They all nodded yes.

In the next instant, they were all over the sky, not great distances, just darting about, as if they were running on a field together. As a result, they didn't run into each other, any more than they would have running in a field. They could see where each was, and thought of going another place.

Then the faeries joined in the fun. They were all golden streaks, all over the sky. The king and queen smiled their approval. They knew that this "game" was very important training. So they let them play, knowing all along that they were preparing themselves for something that was far from a game.

After about one hour of darting about, Herman stopped beside the king. Somewhat out of breath, he asked, "How long does the power of the dust last? This really takes a lot out of you."

Suddenly Shandra was beside him. "How long does the power of the dust last?" he asked again, looking from the king and queen to Shandra.

Then all the rest joined the group. "What's going on?" asked Orria. "You too tired already?"

"Yeah, what's going on?" asked the other pals in unison.

"I want to know how long the power of the dust will last," said Herman, a little impatiently. "I would hate to come falling out of the trees in the middle of the battle!"

"That is really a good question," said Andron. He looked at the king.

The king thought a moment. "We faeries have the dust as part of us. We never run out. We don't know how long it will last with you. It has never been tried."

"That's great," said Cheesey. "We could run out half way over the Atlantic. Nice night for a swim."

"I have an idea," said one of the male faeries that had not said anything yet.

"What's your name?" asked Moussey.

A faerie dressed in green pants, blue shirt, and a yellow jacket responded. "My name is Jorran," responded the faerie. He looked to the king and Andron for approval.

"What is your idea?" asked Shandra, with impatience.

"Well, when one of us is sick, our glow is not as bright. When we get well, it comes back to full brilliance."

"Yes," said Shandra, picking up on Jorran's lead. "And we are not as strong in flight until the full brilliance comes back."

"Yes, but we don't have the brilliance as part of us. You have just loaned it to us," said Cheesey.

"But if our brilliance is still solid, we still have the full power of the dust. Right?" exclaimed Herman with the excitement of discovery.

"It sounds logical," said the king, thoughtfully.

"Then let's test it," said Goossey. "We are doing everything else as an experiment." He looked at the pals and the faeries.

"He's right. You said we have to learn in maybe a couple of days or even hours what takes faeries three years to master," said Moussey. "It's obvious that we are not going to master it as well as they have, but we will have to get by as best we can."

"Three years is the standard amount of time," said the king.

"It has been established by tradition," added the queen.

"Then it may not really be necessary to take that long," said Orria with her usual enthusiasm. "I always thought I was ready for things years before I was allowed to do them." The king and queen had no answer for her.

"Then maybe faeries could learn to fly in several days, if they were allowed to 'spread their wings,'" said Jorran hopefully.

"Maybe not days. But I suppose, seeing how fast the pals have learned, and they aren't even faeries, that it could be less than three years," said the king. "But I will have to discuss it with the elders when we return."

"If we don't get back before the goblins attack, there may not be any reason for discussion," said Greena, bringing everyone back to the reason for all of the flying lessons.

Everyone was suddenly very serious. "No more doubts and wondering," said Herman with his authority voice. "I assume there is a difference between short distance 'thought' movements and long distance travel."

"That is correct," answered Andron. "Long distance travel is also a thought process, but it relates to the speed that you want to move."

Shandra joined in the explanation. "Look to a distant landmark that you can see, and think of going there as fast as you can. The dust will respond."

"It is very close to the speed of the short distance movement, just stretch yourselves, sort of," added Greena.

"Like this?" asked Cheesey, his voice trailing off because he was going off into the distance, extremely fast.

"Catch him!" cried Orria, as she took off after him. All the others followed, seeing Cheesey in the distance, and thinking to catch him. They gained on him and were quickly at his side, traveling so fast that the earth was a blur beneath them.

"Are we going in the right direction?" asked Goossey, surprised that he didn't have to yell. There was no wind.

Shandra saw his wonder. "That is the power of the dust. It puts a protection around us, and yes, we are going in the right direction."

"When you get to the landmark you have in mind, just look to another, and so on. We will be doing it together, so if we stay together, we will get there together," explained Jorran.

"Where do we want to come out on the East Coast," asked Herman, "to start our trek across the Atlantic?"

"I guess that's why Herm is the general," said Cheesey to Moussey. "I never would have thought of something as important as that."

"How do we guide ourselves at night?" asked Goossey.

"By the stars," responded Shandra.

"I have it!" cried Moussey. "We find the Big Dipper, and then the North Star!"

"Yes," said the king. "Always know where the North Star is."

They all got their bearing by the Big Dipper and the North Star, and flew with great speed toward the East Coast.

"We will start across the ocean at about your Washington DC," said Greena.

"You know the way too?" asked Moussey, in admiration.

"Yes, we have all been part of the scout group to see if you were the ones to help us."

"Then the goblins have been a threat for quite a while?" asked Cheesey, hoping they would not be too late.

"Yes. Quite a while. Longer than we want to admit," said Shandra, with fear in her voice.

"They could even be attacking now?" asked Goossey.

"Well, we thought it was not a possibility when we left, but one never knows," said the king.

Herman and his pals could hear the fear in the king's voice as he thought of his people being attacked in his absence.

"Then let's get going. Stretch your landmarks everyone!" yelled Herman, as he and his pals suddenly shot off into the lead. The faeries excitedly caught up to them.

"These are the ones, my dear," quietly said the queen to her husband. "I just hope we are in time."

"See you at the Washington Monument!" cried Moussey. The whole group, pals and faeries, shot exuberantly into the night sky, keeping the guiding star constantly on their left.

CHAPTER SIX

THE JOURNEY BEGINS

"When do you think they will discover the real power of the dust?" Greena asked the Queen.

The queen smiled and answered with a warning wagging of her finger. "Let them become acquainted with stretching themselves. As they learn to stretch, they'll learn how far it is possible to stretch."

"They must learn to handle the power and speed of the dust before knowing its absolute power, or they could injure themselves, or even be killed," added the king.

"Okay, we'll wait," said Orria, joining the king and queen. "But how long can we wait?"

"We must let them master the dust, or they will be of no help when we get to our forest," said the king. "We must let them master the dust."

The queen was encouraging. "You see how they are stretching for the landmarks. They are getting longer and longer."

"That's true. The landmarks are on the horizon now," said Andron, who had just joined the group.

The faeries were allowing Herman and his pals to lead, as they knew the pals had to learn the real power of the dust.

Suddenly Herman stopped and called for all to stop with him. He flew to the king. "Sire, I've noticed two things about our flying together. First, we arrive almost instantly at our destination that we stretch to on the horizon, and second, we arrive as a group, with the leader, who happens to be me." He started to think. His pals looked at each other, trying to figure out what Herman was driving at. It was an interesting sight for any who happened to be looking into the night sky: this group of shining beings high above the earth, suspended in air.

"How often have you been to the Washington Monument?" asked Herman of the king and the other faeries.

"As many times as we have been to your forest," answered Shandra, grinning.

"And many times looking for other forests in your land that would meet our needs," said Andron.

Cheesey was curious about this last statement by Andron. "Did you find any other forests that suited you?"

"We found some beautiful forests," said the king. "You have many, but they were not as easily protected as the one you play in."

"And they were too populated," added Greena.

Goossey became impatient. "These questions can be discussed after we have helped the faeries."

"Yes!" Moussey blurted. "Let's get on with the journey. We don't know how much time we have!"

"You're right, Moussey," said Herman. "But before we go on, I want to go back to my original question. Isn't the monument a landmark?"

"Of course it is," interrupted Goossey. "We four have all seen it. It is one of the most important landmarks in America."

"Am I safe to try what I'm thinking?" Herman asked the king. "We have not flown past the horizon landmarks. We could see there was nothing to run into. Will the dust protect us from things we can't see in advance?"

"Yes!" said Shandra, very excitedly.

"How did you develop it to do that?" asked Herman.

"What is going on here?" asked Goossey, even more impatient. "We've got to get going."

"Wait a minute," said Herman. "If my hunch is right, we will not lose any time, or at least we'll make it up."

"Go ahead and try your theory," said the king.

Herman looked around, noticed a huge river under them. and some lights along its banks and suddenly streaked away. The pals looked at each other in amazement. Shandra, Greena, Orria, clapped their hands. Shandra looked at her mother, the queen. "Do you think he figured it out? What if he makes a mistake?"

"The dust won't let you do that," said Andron.

"Where is he?" asked a concerned Cheesey. The other two pals asked the same question. The group waited impatiently.

"Look! Over there! Off to the left!" exclaimed Goossey.

"It looks like a small point of yellow light, but very bright!" cried Cheesey.

"Let's go see," said Moussey, and they became streaks of golden light.

"I don't quite have it down, do I?" said Herman to the king. "I thought I had my bearings better than this. I almost missed you."

"Well, we must all learn absolute precision," said Shandra, smiling with great satisfaction at what she knew Herman had just done.

"If someone doesn't tell me what is going on . . .," said Cheesey.

"Herman just used the ultimate power of the dust," said Greena. "He went to the Washington Monument, or some landmark in Washington. Right, Herman?"

"I went to the monument all right," said Herman with great pride. "Some of the folks there think they saw someone from another planet though."

"You went to the Washington Monument?" asked Goossey.

"Come on," said Cheesey. "That's still too far away. You can't get there as fast as that."

"You were only gone for a few minutes," said Moussey. "No one can travel that fast. Not even in a jet plane."

"Yes, they can! With the faerie dust you can!" said Orria, clapping her hands in joy because of Herman's discovery.

"You did it, Moussey, when you went home a little while ago," said the king. "You moved at the speed of thought because it was not very far."

"A distance from here to Washington does not go at the same speed of thought," said Herman, "but I was going so fast, I couldn't see the earth passing beneath me."

"If he was going that fast, how come he didn't hit something?" asked Goossey, still doubting.

"I felt myself moving from side to side. I guess the dust was helping me avoid things in the way. Right?"

"Right!" said Shandra.

"The dust has great powers this way. We have simply learned to use it," added the queen.

"We don't know how fast we travel over long distances like you did, Herman," said Orria. "We just know that we must have a very good picture in our minds as to where we are going, or we can get lost."

"Has anyone gotten lost—permanently?" asked Cheesey, not really wanting to hear the answer.

"Yes," answered the king. "But the two were very young faeries and didn't really have a good picture in their minds of where they were going."

"As a matter of fact, they were going to too small of a place, and they couldn't get a very big picture of it in their minds," said Andron.

"Too small to get a good picture?" asked Moussey.

"Yes, too small. They were traveling to a certain tree in the forest many miles away. We assume they not only didn't find the tree, but didn't have a good picture of where they started from."

"We never saw them again."

"They were not very nice faeries, anyway," said Greena.

"Greena! It's not polite to talk of other faeries that way," corrected the queen.

"We know that, Mamma, but they were not very nice. Rebellious is the word!" said Shandra.

"They had their problems, it is true. But we must be careful how we speak of our brother and sister faeries. It can cause division in our kingdom and I will not allow it. You know that, Shandra," said the king, with authority that only a king could use.

"I'm sorry, father," said a very humbled Shandra.

"I'm sorry too," said Greena.

"It is a fact that we do not know what happened to them. Maybe they did just run away," joined the queen. "But if one is careful in traveling with the dust, it can be done with great precision."

"If you're not sure, stay with the group. The dust works with a group as well as for individuals," said Orria.

"If one person knows the way, the others will just be taken along," said Andron.

"Do we need to practice like Herman did?" asked Goossey, "or can we get on to your kingdom before the war is over?"

"We can travel short distances quite well. You said that is what we would need in battle," said Moussey.

"But we don't know where we are going when we cross the ocean. So we can travel as a group. Right?" asked Cheesey.

"We have been so involved in your learning the power of the dust that we let the danger slip away a little," said the king. "You are right, Goossey. We thought you would need the time to learn the long distance power of the dust, but we really don't have time."

"We know the power now. We just don't know fully how to use it," said Herman. "So maybe we had better learn that part of the power later. Let's get with it!"

"Lead on, sire. We'll be glad to be part of your group. I think it is called a captive audience!" laughed Cheesey. They all had a good laugh. The king then pictured the faerie forest in his mind; all the group got into tight formation, and off they went.

"We'll gain some altitude," said the king. "Less air resistance."

"And less worry of people on the earth seeing us and being frightened," said Andron.

"May I be the lead person, sire?" asked a person no one had heard much from.

The king looked at the queen and the other faeries. Then he smiled. "Yes, Jorran. You may be the leader. But make sure you get a good picture."

"I will!" smiled Jorran, grinning so much that the pals thought his mouth would split apart.

They had traveled very fast to get to the high altitude.

"We got here at the same speed that I traveled," said Herman. "How did you do that?"

"I merely pictured a star, then we moved toward it. Then I thought to stop, so we did," answered the king.

"Okay, Jorran. Got the picture?" Jorran nodded. "Then let's go!"

The group moved together. Anyone on earth looking into the night sky would think they were seeing a falling star, leaving a beautiful golden trail behind it.

CHAPTER SEVEN

NEAR TRAGEDY

The world below was a blur for only a moment, then it all turned black. The group was moving at extreme speed, but still able to carry on conversations among themselves. "Where did the world go?" asked Moussey.

"We are over the ocean," answered Orria. "It doesn't give off much light. It appears as a big black hole."

"If we were lower, you could hear the waves. But we don't have time for that this trip."

"Yeah. Maybe next time," Cheesey murmured quietly.

Everyone knew what he meant. None knew what lay ahead of them in the battle to come with the goblins. Would they come back? Would they have the chance to share the beauties of flight with their newfound friends?

Suddenly Moussey shot away from the group. "Look, I can still keep speed with you and investigate by myself. I'm really learning about the dust!" Suddenly the glow that the dust was giving him went dim.

"The dust is fading on him!" cried the queen. "Support the other pals. It will probably start to fade on them too!"

Before the queen had spoken, Greena, streaked after Moussey, who had now completely lost the dust. She could just barely see him as a black dot falling toward the ocean, thousands of feet below. She knew that she must stop him or he would die when he hit the water. She had to get under him and support him with her dust and slow him down gradually. He fell faster and faster, making it difficult for her to get a fix on him for an instant move to his side. It was dark; only the moonlight allowed her to distinguish him from the night sky. Suddenly Andron, Jorran, Shandra, Orria, and ten other faeries sent by the king, appeared at her side. "He still has some dust influence on him, or he would be falling faster!" yelled Jorran.

"We must stop him gradually!" she cried.

Moussey was turning end over end as he fell toward the black ocean waters below. He knew he was going to die if he hit the water. He had made a foolish mistake in going away from the group. Looking up he saw several streaks of light coming toward him. "How can I tell them where I am?" Then he remembered the flashlight that all of the pals carried in their pockets. "I hope it hasn't fallen out," he said to himself. He reached in his pockets. It was still there. He could hear the waves below him. "Must be rough water, or I'm closer than I want to be," he thought.

He turned on the light and shined it into the night sky. "There he is!" yelled Greena. She and Andron moved with the speed of the dust to a point below Moussey, hoping that point would not be in the ocean. The other rescuers followed.

The rest of the group watched helplessly from their vantage point thousands of feet in the air. "Let's slowly descend to see if we can be of any help when they rescue him," counseled the Queen.

Several faeries started to move their wings to produce extra dust before they were below Moussey. By the time they got below him, he was completely enveloped in the dust. They could hear the waves. Moussey felt his descent become slower. "We can't slow him down anymore. He'll be in the water!" yelled Andron.

"Catch him and throw him up at the same time!" cried Greena. "He may have slowed down enough and it may cushion the fall enough. We have to try it!"

With their combined thoughts, they intensified the power of the dust. As Moussey fell into it, the faeries gathered under him and threw him upward. He was jarred a little, as the dust had not completely stopped him, but he was not hurt.

Moussey felt the power of the dust on him and was able to keep himself in the air. The group of friends looked below them. They had caught Moussey only a few feet above the water.

Suddenly the others were at their sides. The whole group was again enveloped in the dust. "I guess we learned that the dust will not be permanent," said the king. "Let's give the other pals an extra supply and get on with our journey."

Very embarrassed, Moussey quietly apologized to the group. "I'm really sorry for being so dumb. But I felt that I could do it."

"You did do it," encouraged Jorran. "You were flying with us. You just didn't know you were going to lose the power of the dust at that moment."

"We will need to watch these pals very closely when we get into battle. We don't know how long the dust will last under that kind of stress and excitement," said the queen.

Suddenly they were again thousands of feet above the dark ocean, headed for the faeries' home forest. Everyone was silent, hoping they were not too late.

CHAPTER EIGHT

THE HOME FOREST

In a very short time, the darkness of the ocean became the blur of the lights of land again. It was impossible for Herman and his pals to distinguish any landmarks as they were traveling too fast. In another very short time, they had only the black hole of the Mediterranean below them. They turned north and the land was again a blur beneath them. They knew they were heading north to the great home forest of the faeries. They were glad that Jorran had taken them so high to start with, for they crossed many high mountains. The sun had risen. They could see a white blur that they assumed was snow. The pals noticed they didn't feel cold. They were again amazed at the protective power of the dust. Suddenly they stopped above a very high, snow-capped mountain.

"Why have we stopped?" asked Goossey. "I don't see any forest beneath us."

"We are so high that you couldn't see the forest anyway," said Shandra. "It is on the other side of this mountain range. We get this picture in our minds when we travel home from other places in the world."

"Then we slowly drift down to our forest," said the queen.

"I don't think we should take the time to drift slowly," said Jorran. "We had better go fast. I have a particular part of the forest canopy pictured in my mind. May I, sire?"

The king nodded, and the group suddenly moved to a point above a very deep dark green forest. The pals could not see into the forest.

"The forest canopy is so thick that no light escapes from our kingdom," said the king.

"If any light escaped, our kingdom would be discovered at night," explained Andron.

"You see," said the king, "the faerie dust gives our kingdom light also."

The pals looked at each other in wonder and awe. "When do we get to see the kingdom?" asked Moussey, almost reverently.

"I think we should approach slowly," counseled Jorran, "just in case."

"Good idea. Let's go to a point halfway between the top of the forest and the floor and see if anything is happening," directed Shandra.

The group slowly descended into the forest. "We will have to separate," Orria told the pals.

"We cannot stay in a group anymore. The forest is too thick," added Greena.

They separated, but kept each other in view.

Before they went down into the forest, Goossey said to the pals, "There doesn't seem to be an end to this forest." They all looked around and agreed. They also noticed that the forest was a beautiful, dark green color, such as they had never seen before. As they dropped down into the canopy, each of the pals stayed near one of the faeries, so they wouldn't get lost.

"This is going to take some time to learn," said Herman. "This place is so vast. How will we ever find our way around?"

"You will learn," said Greena. "Let's hope that the goblins have the same problem, only they won't have us as guides."

The trees were hundreds of feet high. Halfway down, they stopped descending and started to weave around the trees, all heading in the same direction.

"We still can't see the floor of the forest," said Moussey. All they could see were the thick leaves and limbs of the trees.

"We are trying to hear something," cautioned the king. "I hear nothing. Let's go down farther toward the floor of the forest."

They dropped slowly to a point where if someone were on the floor, they would not be able to see them in the trees, unless they knew exactly where to look.

"Hey! Isn't that the same kind of grass as in the glen back home?" asked Herman. There were beautiful flowers similar to what they had seen in the faerie glen, but many more. The bark of the trees was of the same beautiful browns, dark and light.

Goossey felt the bark. "This bark is the same as the trees in the glen back home."

"Many of the trees are the same kind," said the queen. "There are many more varieties in this forest."

"Are we in the middle of your forest?" asked Cheesey.

"No, this is only the edge of the forest," said Orria. "We are heading into the center, where we live."

"Shouldn't there be guards?" asked Herman.

"There are some at the very edge of the forest," said Andron.

"How many?" asked Herman.

"Five," answered Andron, somewhat embarrassed. "I guess there should be more?"

"You should have them placed at intervals from the edge clear to the center," counseled Herman.

Just then they heard Shandra cry out. She was slightly ahead of the group.

"What's wrong?" cried Jorran.

"Look!" Everyone could hear the fear in her voice.

All looked down where she was pointing. They all had to keep themselves from crying out. The grass was trampled and black. The black trail led off into the forest. They all could see where it went and from where it came. Luckily, it did not lead into the center of the forest.

"Goblins!" said the king.

"But they don't seem to know where they are going," said Andron, hopefully.

Herman took over the leadership. "Jorran, you and Orria follow the trail that way, and, Greena, you and Moussey follow it the other way. Scout the trails until you see the beginning or the goblins, and watch out for Moussey losing the dust. The rest of us will go on to the center of the kingdom."

The faeries looked at each other and smiled. "We have done the right thing," said the king to the queen.

"I have a good idea," said Goossey. "Why not give us a supply of the dust right now, just in case. We have come quite a distance since you renewed the dust."

"There has to be a way to know when to renew the dust on them," said Orria to the queen.

"I don't think there is a way," said the queen. "Remember the dust just suddenly got dim and disappeared with Moussey over the ocean?"

"But he was not as brilliant as the dust should have made him," said Andron.

"That's true," said Herman. "Then we have to always have a faerie with one of us. If we get dim, or can't fly anymore, there will be someone there to help us."

"It's kind of inconvenient," said the king, "but it is the only way until we learn more of how the dust affects big people."

"Okay, everyone. Off to your scouting and the rest of us to the center of the forest to organize the faerie army!" commanded Herman.

After the pals had received a new supply of the dust, Jorran and Orria went their way and Greena and Moussey went their way. As Herman and the rest of the faeries started toward the center of the forest, Herman told them of his plans. "We must fight carefully, in open spaces if possible. Otherwise, when we are dodging the goblins, we may hit a tree and hurt ourselves and then be at the mercy of the goblins. This goes for pals and faeries."

"You're right, Herman," said Shandra. "We are not used to moving fast inside the forest. It is very dense, and moving fast could be dangerous."

"But will we always be able to find an open space?" asked Cheesey. "If we can't, what do we do then?"

"And are there open spaces in this dense forest?" asked Goossey.

"Yes, there are many," answered the queen. "You just have to know where they are."

"Well then. When we are not in the open spaces, we will just have to be more careful," said Herman.

"This is going to be complicated at times," said Andron, "but we will just have to do it."

"We will have time for a council with your faeries, Andron, before the battle. Especially if the goblins stay lost for a while," said Herman.

"If they are not headed for the center of the forest, then we need to organize and attack them before they find their way to the center of our kingdom," said the king.

"Too bad the dust will not avoid all of these trees as we travel like it did coming here," said Cheesey, thoughtfully.

"It does not avoid things as fast as the trees would come in the forest," said Andron. "In the sky there are not that many things, and there is time enough for the dust to send us around them."

"Andron is right," said the king. "We have to fly by our normal sight when we are in the forest. It is much slower. The dust does not give us the power to travel through things."

"Well, hopefully this war will teach us what we need to know about moving in the forest at great speeds," said Shandra.

"Hopefully, we will never have to use what we learn again," responded the queen.

Everyone nodded in silent agreement as they flew on to the center of the forest and the main dwelling place of the faeries.

CHAPTER NINE

DISCOVERIES

Greena and Moussey weaved their way around trees, keeping the black trail in sight. "It is terrible what they have done to the forest floor," said Moussey.

"I guess the grass is not used to strangers walking on it," said Greena. "You know, I would like to feel the black grass, to find out what the goblins really do to it."

"It would be risky," said Moussey. "But if I stay up in the trees, I could see if someone is coming."

"On second thought, maybe you should touch the blackened grass. It might not be good for me."

"Good thinking," Moussey agreed as he glided to the forest floor, being careful not to land on the blackened trail.

Greena watched both directions for any goblins. As Moussey looked at the grass, he quickly noticed that the grass seemed dead, like it had been burned away. The ground underneath was black, like it had also been burned. He carefully touched just the edge of the blackened area. It was very cool. The green healthy grass he was standing on was warm. Then he touched the center of the blackened trail. It was very cold. "This ground and the grass are not used to the touch of the goblin feet."

"Trade me places," said Greena. "You come up and watch. I want to feel it."

"I don't think you will like it," warned Moussey.

"I must know!" she insisted.

"Okay, here I come," responded Moussey, gliding up into the trees.

Greena slowly descended to the green grass. She could feel the cold from the trail. "It is cold," she said.

"If you can feel it without touching it, then don't touch it!" cried Moussey.

Greena was too curious. She flew to the center of the trail and reached out her hand to touch the center of the blackened trail. "Ohhhh!"

Greena's cry brought Moussey to the forest floor dangerously fast. Luckily he went straight down to her side, not sideways into trees. Greena was sitting on the green grass, holding her arm, obviously in great pain.

"What's wrong?" asked Moussey, seeing the pain and fear in Greena's eyes. "What happened? What did you do?"

"I touched the center of the trail. It was so cold. The cold went up my arm. I have never felt such cold before!"

"Is your arm still cold?"

"Yes, but it is coming back to normal. But not fast enough for me." She smiled a little smile of pain and embarrassment.

"You were very foolish to do that. You didn't know what would happen. What if it had frozen your arm or your whole body? You could have died!" Moussey was very upset and afraid and sounded angry.

Greena looked at him with fear in her eyes. "How can we fight creatures that leave our land so cold that it takes away our strength? What if I had fallen on to the trail with my whole body?"

"Hopefully you would have been removed before you received any permanent damage."

"But what if one of us is unconscious and then falls on the trail?"

"Why did it affect you and not me?" asked a bewildered Moussey.

"We are more sensitive to cold than you are. We don't live with it like you do. We are always protected by the dust. It insulates us against the outside world."

"Then the goblins destroyed the insulation of the dust on the forest floor."

"Maybe the floor is not used to such rough treatment. The dust does give things a power of their own. The floor may not like what the goblins felt like and it just gave up its heat."

"If it is used to the protection of the dust like you are, that would make sense. It just can't be touched by such creatures as goblins and continue to give off its life giving heat. So it went cold. I'm used to cold, so it didn't bother me. You aren't, so you were affected more than I was. But why did it go up your arm?"

"Maybe the goblins carry a power of their own, so different from mine that I cannot bear to touch what they touch."

"Am I so close to that power?" asked Moussey. "The bad power of the goblins?"

"No," said Greena, thinking about what she could say to her troubled friend. "I know I am much smaller, and that has something to do with it, but I don't think it is the whole reason. I just don't know the answer."

"Will the others discover this negative power of the goblins before some of them find out the hard way?" asked Moussey.

"I don't know, but we have to scout this trail to the end, or the beginning, and then get back to the kingdom center as fast as possible."

"Okay, no more detours," said Moussey, flying off through the trees. He quickly turned around. "Can you fly?"

"I think so," said Greena quietly. She glided into the air. "I'm okay. Let's get going!"

The two friends flew through the forest without any more curious detours. "Are we headed into or out of the forest?" asked Moussey.

"We're headed toward the edge of the forest, the edge that borders the mountains."

"Then we're headed for the place where the goblins live. Right?"

"Right!"

They noticed something as they flew. The trail was not as wide as it had been. "Is the trail getting more narrow?" asked Moussey.

"Yes. I wonder what is going on," answered Greena.

Moussey was curious. "I've got to find out. You stay up in the trees. The trail doesn't hurt me." He landed and immediately noticed on close observation that the grass was growing back over the trail. "The grass is growing back over the trail. It is covering the bad power of the goblins!"

Greena flew to his side. "It is not as cold either."

"You shouldn't have come down here!" cried Moussey, a little put out at Greena's foolish curiosity.

"This is marvelous!" exclaimed Greena, ignoring Moussey's warning. "It is not as cold to me. The grass is already healing itself! The floor of the forest must still have strength in it. It just couldn't stand the touch of the goblin feet!"

"You're probably right, but when the floor is cold, it is very dangerous, maybe even deadly to a faerie!"

"The edge of the forest is so close now. I think the goblins passed here and are going the other direction. We must get back to the center and warn the others of our discoveries!"

"But what if more goblins come from the mountain?" asked Moussey. "Did all of them come or are there still more coming in a second army?"

"How will we find out?" Greena was afraid of what Moussey was suggesting.

"The only way we will know is to find the entrance to the goblin mountain and wait. We could set up some faeries along the top of the forest canopy and use the extreme speed of the dust to fly to the next person and send messages by relay. You have to go back and set up the relay system. We can't let the goblins bring out reinforcements without our knowing it!"

"But we don't know where the entrance is!" she warned.

"We'll have to keep following the trail until we find it."

Moussey was thinking. "You must get a solid picture of the outside of the forest where the trail comes out and then fly to the center of the forest, find the canopy above the center of the kingdom, picture it in your mind and then come back. I'll be waiting. Then we can fly on to the entrance of the goblin mountain and I'll stand guard and wait until I have to send a signal."

"But what if you lose the power of the dust while you are waiting?"

"Then you'll have to be here or send another faerie to be with me, just in case. Let's find the entrance. You can use that as your starting point and go from there to the center of the forest."

Greena did not like the idea, but she knew that Moussey was right. They must know if there were still more goblins to come. Maybe this was only a scouting party. The rest of the army may still be at the mountain. "We must tell someone what our plans are and what we have discovered," said Greena.

"But I have to get looking for the entrance. What if the trail *was* made by a scouting party and the main army *is* still at the mountain?"

Greena was pleased that they were both thinking the same thing about the possibility of a scouting party. "Jorran and Orria will discover if it is only a scouting party and then send word to the kingdom center."

"But then no one will know that we are spying on the entrance," said Moussey, a little impatiently.

"They both thought about what to do. "I have it!" cried Moussey. "I'll get a picture of this place. You get a picture of this place and then fly above the forest canopy to the kingdom. You will fly too slowly down in the forest."

"We don't fly above the canopy," answered Greena. "We have always flown down in the forest and just enjoyed the beauty of it."

"You can't find the forest center by flying above the canopy?" asked Moussey in disbelief.

"We never needed knowledge of the canopy before."

"Well, it is time to learn!" said Moussey firmly. "I'm going up to the mountain. I'll come back here every ten minutes to see if you have returned. I can follow the trail up the mountain, I hope." He said these last words as he flew off up the trail.

"I guess I had better get on with my part of the plan," Greena said to herself. Then she remembered that she had not renewed Moussey's dust before he left. "No time now. I must get to the center of the forest." She flew off toward the center of the forest, hoping to get some pictures in her mind of the canopy to help her cross it as quickly as possible. She also hoped Moussey would not run out of dust before she returned.

CHAPTER TEN

GREENA CROSSES THE FOREST

Greena decided that she would have to let Moussey get along as best he could. He would be careful, she hoped. She must get to the others and report. She pictured in her mind the forest and the path, and looked for a point of reference toward the center of the forest. Finding a somewhat taller tree, she moved. She made several mistakes in her reckoning to the center of the forest. She decided to drop into the forest to see if she was indeed near the center. "Oh, I wish we were better prepared for flying above the canopy," she exclaimed to herself. "Then I would know where I am." Greena had forgotten in her haste that the faeries did not go about in the forest at night either. Far from the center, it would get dark. No moonlight and no starlight could penetrate to the forest floor. As she descended, far too fast for the conditions, she hit a large tree limb; she was knocked unconscious and fell toward the floor of the forest. If the thick branches had not stopped her fall, she would have been dashed to her death on the forest floor, hundreds of feet below.

Cradled in the trees until she regained consciousness, she realized immediately what had happened. Yelling at herself for her stupidity, she rose to the top of the canopy. Darkness had fallen. Suddenly she saw a bright streak that seemed to be moving in her direction, but very far away. Her forest was a massive protection for the faerie kingdom, but a terrible barrier to a lost faerie, far from the center light. She shook herself and made a decision. No more waiting. She had a report to make. She must move and move now.

Greena suddenly became a streak of silver gold splitting the night sky above the black canopy of her forest home as she flew toward the golden streak in the distance.

CHAPTER ELEVEN

SCOUTS

Jorran and Orria flew as fast as was safe in the dense trees. They flew faster than Greena and Moussey had, as they were more used to going around the trees. They had done this as a game when they were young faeries, a dangerous game, but the faeries learned to get through the forest quite well. They were unable to go as fast as they might, as they had to concentrate on the trail instead of the trees in front of them.

"The trail is still staying on the edge of the forest," said Orria, somewhat encouraged.

"Yes, the goblins seem to have a bad sense of direction," responded Jorran.

"Lucky for us," said Orria. "But they are far enough into the forest that they can't see the edge. They don't know they are not going into the center."

"We are assuming they are ahead of us," said Jorran. "What if they are going the other direction, where Greena and Moussey are?"

"I hope we find out soon," said Orria.

The two faeries flew on as fast as they could. Suddenly they both came to a halt and listened carefully.

"You heard it too?" whispered Orria.

"Yes," whispered Jorran. "Let's go up into the trees."

They flew on, just within sight of the trail. The noises got louder and louder. At last they could distinguish voices, mean, rough, and angry voices. They could not understand any of the words. The goblins appeared below them. They were sitting in a circle in a small clearing in the forest. They had cut down one of the trees and built a small fire. "They cut the trees!" whispered Orria.

"Let's go down for a closer look," said Jorran. Orria was afraid of the idea, but stayed at Jorran's side as they slowly descended toward the goblins. The faeries came to rest on some shrubbery far enough away from the goblins so they wouldn't see the brilliance of their dust. Fear of discovery caused the faeries to think hard to be less brilliant, and they noticed that it worked. The brilliance seemed to close in around them and get quite dim.

"Did you think what I thought?" asked Jorran.

"What, to be as dim as I can?" asked Orria.

"We must remember to tell the others about this power of the dust."

Orria saw her first goblin up close. Jorran had seen them before. They were short, about half the height of Herman and his pals, but very stout, with arms quite big and short, stubby legs. Their legs reminded Jorran of small tree trunks. They carried clubs made from small tree limbs. Their clothing consisted of short pants, about midthigh, and rough hide jackets fastened in front by loops over bone sewn onto the jackets.

The jackets were open at the throat and along with the pants, dirty gray in color.

"They look awfully strong," commented Orria.

"If they hit us with one of those clubs, we'll be dead," added Jorran. "They are only about half as tall as Herman and his pals, but they are just as strong I would guess."

"They are so much bigger than we are," said Orria. "How are we going to fight creatures as large as that?"

"Herman has to know what we are seeing," said Jorran. "Do you notice anything else?"

Orria thought a moment. "There are only a few of them. This is only a scouting party."

"And the grass is not blackened in front of them. They are coming from the direction Greena and Moussey went."

"Jorran, where is the main army?"

"Not here yet. These guys are scouting out the forest. Maybe so the main army can find the kingdom. We must get a picture of the canopy. We can fly faster above the forest than through it, and we must get to the center as quickly as possible."

"You have more experience than I have in using the canopy to fly," said Orria. "I'll stay with the goblins and you get to Herman and the king."

"But how will I know where you are?"

"I'll come to the canopy every once in a while. Just watch for me!"

"Watch for you! Over the vastness of this forest? That's impossible!"

"We have no choice, Jorran. You must warn Herman." Jorran hesitated. "You must go now!" insisted Orria, with authority in her voice that made Jorran smile, but he knew she was right.

CHAPTER TWELVE

THE KINGDOM

Arriving at the top of the forest, Jorran looked for some trees taller than their neighbors. Looking in the direction of the center of the forest, he spied one. He immediately moved to it, then another, and so on. After four such moves, he descended into the forest to find out how close he was to the center. Then he went back to the top and continued his search. After four more moves, he dropped into the forest again. He was now very close to the center. He could tell by the light coming from the kingdom; it spread through the forest, getting brighter as one approached the center. Once more to the top of the forest, two more moves, down into the forest again, he was right over the center. Jorran had carefully remembered all of the treemarks he had used to get to the center. "I wonder what they will look like at night?" he asked himself. He didn't have long to wonder.

A faerie appeared at his side. Jorran recognized his friend Shellane. Shellane was dressed all in blue with flowing blond hair cut to shoulder length.

"We have been watching for you, Jorran. We have instructions to take you immediately to Herman."

"How did you know I would come this way?" asked Jorran.

"We are stationed all around the center. Herman has been busy organizing us."

"Take me to him. We have a great deal of organizing to do to fight these creatures."

Shellane led him to the center of the clearing next to the king's dwelling. Jorran realized, for the first time, that Herman and his pals would not fit into the faerie homes. The clearing next to the king's dwelling was the largest in the forest. Herman and his two pals took up the whole area. Faeries were sitting on the grass, all around the pals. The king and queen were perched on Herman and Goossey's knees as they sat cross-legged in conference. When Jorran arrived, they all stopped and listened to his report.

Every part of the report gave them cause for concern. They wondered at the blackened trail, the clubs, and the strange language; only the king and a few scouts had heard the goblins speak. They sorrowed at the tree the goblins had cut down for fire. There was hope in the fact that it was only a small scouting party; the army had not left. Then they were afraid for Greena and Moussey.

"Your report brings many questions to this council we cannot answer," said the king. "You say Orria is just watching?"

"Orria will not be able to just watch," said a faerie sitting on Goossey's shoulder.

"I know," said Jorran, "but I knew how to move over the top of the forest better than Orria. We had no choice."

"You were correct in coming, Jorran," comforted Herman. "This gives us more to work with. It takes away some of the guesswork in our plans."

"But what will we do with such creatures in battle?" asked Shandra.

"We must stop the scouts from returning to the main goblin army," said Herman. "Then we must find out the size of the army before it comes."

"We don't even know where it will come from," said Cheesey.

"We know they will come from the mountains," said Andron. "But we don't know where they will enter the forest."

"Greena and Moussey know that by now," said Goossey. "All we have to do is find them."

The group looked at each other, then at Goossey. "Not an easy thing to do," admitted Goossey, rather quietly.

"We could send faeries all along the mountain side of the forest until they find either the goblins or Moussey and Greena," said another faerie sitting on Goossey's other knee.

"Goossey is right!" said Herman. "Moussey and Greena know where the trail comes into the forest and I'm sure they are finding a way right now to get the information to us. We must travel at the speed of the dust to the edge of the forest!"

"We have never done it before," said the queen.

"Jorran, how did you get here?" asked Andron.

"I flew above the canopy."

"At the speed of the dust?" asked Shellane.

"Yes. Using trees as landmarks and moving instantly from one to another. But even that was too slow. We must extend the distance between the landmark trees."

"But you can get us back to where Orria is?" asked Shandra hopefully.

Jorran bowed his head. "I didn't take a treemark from where I started. I can get us close to her, but not right at the spot where she and the goblins are."

The thought of Orria being alone in the company of the goblins made them all shudder with fear.

"We have no time to lose!" said Herman, suddenly taking over command of the conversation. "Your Majesty, who can we send to the mountain edge of the forest? We will need several faeries."

"More than several, I fear," said the queen. "You do not know the size of the forest."

"I want them to be able to see each other as they scout the edge of the forest."

"We will need many, perhaps one hundred," said Shandra, looking at her father for approval of the number.

"We can start with that many," said the king, "but aren't we a little premature? Why not wait for Moussey and Greena? They will lead us straight to the trail, then we can follow it to the right place on the mountain."

Silence followed as all thought about the king's suggestion.

"You're right, Your Majesty," said Herman. "Jorran, you must lead us to the point nearest to where you left Orria. We must find a way to stop that scouting party!"

"I hope Orria is all right!" blurted a faerie on Cheesey's shoulder. She was dress in yellow with blue shoes and short brown hair. Her name was Falslevia.

"We all share your fears, Falslevia," comforted the king.

"She is one of my best friends! She has to be all right!"

"Then let's get going!" cried Goossey. "Give us a new supply of the dust." He stood up and dislodged the faeries on his knees. The king smiled as the faeries rose above the pals and gave them a renewed dusting.

"I know you must be tired, Jorran," said Herman, but . . ."

"I'm okay," Jorran responded. "Let's get going!" He smiled at Goossey as he rose toward the canopy.

"We must have a large group of our people," said Herman to the king.

All the faeries in the clearing began to rise, perhaps two hundred.

"Fifty will do until we get our treemarks settled," said Herman. The king quickly chose fifty to go. The rest drifted to the ground, disappointed.

"You'll get your chance, unfortunately!" cried Herman as he rose out of sight into the thick forest greenery.

It wasn't until they arrived at the forest canopy that they learned that night had fallen.

"You really can't tell if it is night or day when you are down in the forest," observed Cheesey.

"We live in constant light," said Shandra. "Few of us know what darkness looks like."

Cheesey noticed the wonder on the faces of many of the faeries. "These must be those that have never seen darkness." Shandra nodded.

Herman gathered everyone around him. "Jorran will lead."

All looked to Jorran. He was looking with wonder at the top of the forest at night. "I was afraid of this," he said, doubtfully. "Give me a moment. I came in the daylight. The forest is much different at night."

He observed carefully the canopy of the forest. "I think I see the first treemark. Let's go!" The whole group moved with blurring speed to Jorran's first treemark.

"Yes! This is it!" he exclaimed joyfully. Confidently he looked to the next treemark. The group, thanks to Jorran's memory of treemarks, arrived at the last one before looking for Orria. "I don't know what to do now," he lamented, discouraged and fearful for his friend.

CHAPTER THIRTEEN

ORRIA'S COURAGE

As Jorran slowly glided to the forest canopy, Orria was amazed that his brilliance was so dim. She soon lost sight of him. The gruff voices of the goblins reminded her of where she was, and the danger she was in. "What am I going to do?" she asked herself. "And how am I ever going to let Jorran know where I am when he comes back." She waited, watched, and tried to understand what the goblins were saying.

They laughed a lot, and drank out of some kind of container made of a material she had never seen before.

She decided that she would wait until they fell asleep or moved on. Whatever they were drinking had an interesting effect. They got very loud and started to push each other around. Orria was glad there were only five of them. "They smell so bad, I don't think I could stand it if there were more of them," she thought to herself. Even their voices were uncomfortable for her. They hurt her ears. "I'm sure all of the faeries, except the scouts the king placed at the mountain edge of the forest, are completely unaware of this kind of being. I have never heard their language. Their smell stings my nose and eyes. Their voices hurt my ears. They are strange and frightening!" she continued to think to herself.

Suddenly one of the goblins pushed another one hard into a tree. He fell forward on his face and didn't get up. Orria didn't know whether he was dead or just unconscious. Another yelled at the one who had pushed his companion into the tree and hit him with his club. He fell over and didn't move. The one with the club glared at the other two. They yelled at him and sat down and leaned against a tree. Soon all three were asleep, the two now lying down and the one with the club leaning against a tree with his head down on his chest. Orria waited until she was sure they were sleeping soundly.

Slowly she glided into the glade and hovered above their clubs. "Could I lift one of these?" she asked herself. Then she realized how foolish it would be to try. She glided over to the containers of their drinks. They smelled so terrible she suddenly got sick. She quickly flew away where she could get some fresh air. The sick feeling left after a few minutes and she courageously flew back to the goblins.

"Will faerie dust move them?" she thought. She moved her wings above one of the clubs; a little dust fell on the club. Nothing happened. "Maybe I can lift it now," she thought. She flew next to the club. It was many times her size. She was right next to the goblins. They looked much larger than they had from the air. "We can't fight them! They are so huge. What are we going to do?" She reached for the club, put her tiny hand under it, and lifted. It moved slightly. She glided above it and gave it some more dust from her wings, went to it and lifted again. She was able to move it. But the wood was rough and cut her hand. The club suddenly got very heavy; she noticed the dust falling off it just before she let go of it. It hit the ground with a loud thud. The goblins were suddenly awakened. Orria flew off into the underbrush. The one who had hit the other yelled at the one next to the club Orria had dropped. The one by the club picked it up and yelled back. The two goblins circled each other. The ones who had been hit earlier were still on the ground where they had fallen, and the one remaining watched the other two circling.

Suddenly one rushed at the other, swinging his club. The one under attacked swung his club. Their clubs smashed together with a loud crunching sound and one broke in two. The goblin with the broken club looked at his club and turned to run just as the other one hit him in the head. The one watching yelled something and then fell silent. Soon they were asleep again.

They made horrible sounds when they slept. Orria glided into the glade. "More dust," she thought. She moved her wings vigorously over one of the clubs, lifted it and rose into the air. She pushed it to a spot several feet from the glade, dropped it, and went back for another. With a lot more dust, all of the clubs, except the broken one were hidden away from the trail. Her hands were bleeding.

The fire was almost out. "I must find a way to signal Jorran now," she thought to herself. "Herman must know that we can move the clubs." She was very tired but flew as fast as she could to the top of the forest. Her hands were hurting her; she had never known such pain. She had bumped into trees while flying too fast as a young faerie, but this pain was new to her. She looked down into the forest, but could see nothing. "I hope the goblins can't see this," she thought. She rose a few feet above the top of the trees and made herself as brilliant as she could. Suddenly she got dizzy. "I guess I overdid it with those clubs." She lost consciousness and fell into the cradling limbs of the tree tops, a small, dim form almost lost in the leaves of the great trees that held her.

CHAPTER FOURTEEN

ORRIA AND GREENA ARE FOUND

Orria made herself brilliant just as Jorran began to lead Herman and the others across the forest.

"There she is! Somebody lock on to that!"

"Take us Goossey! You saw it!" cried Cheesey.

"Can you do it?" asked Andron.

The group moved toward where Goossey had seen the point of light. They moved quickly at first, then more slowly as the point of light disappeared. "She must have flared and then gone dim," cautioned Shellane.

"She must be very tired," said Falslevia.

A faerie in the lead of the group cried out. "There she is!"

They all looked to the top of the forest. A very dim light could be seen. Just as they were about to move to her, a streak of light came from the mountain edge of the forest. All stopped. They knew it must be Greena. Both faeries were found. The joy of all made the group more brilliant above the thick, dark tops of the trees.

Then Cheesey noticed, as Greena arrived at the group. "She is alone. Moussey is not with her."

The brilliance of the group suddenly went dim as they descended to pick up their comrade from the cradle of the forest and prepared to listen to Greena's report.

CHAPTER FIFTEEN

HERMAN TAKES CHARGE

O rria looked up into the faces of her friends. They had carefully taken her to the floor of the forest. Herman had sent out the scouts to the areas near the edge of the forest with Jorran and Greena, Greena taking them to the edge she had pictured in her mind. "The Goblins!" Orria cried out in terror. "We can lift their clubs with the dust. But it takes a lot of it." The king told her what had happened to the goblins after she had been found lying in the canopy of the forest.

"When we found you, we noticed your hands. You flinched when we touched them, even though you were unconscious. The pain brought you out of it. We wanted to take you back to the kingdom center for some help, but you refused. You had to make your report, and we really couldn't risk the time. So we sent someone back to get some healing oils and you made your report at the top of the trees. When we heard that the goblins were almost directly below us, Herman went immediately accompanied by Jorran, Andron, and Shellane."

"Let us move very slowly and quietly," cautioned Herman. "If they are still asleep, they will be easier to handle."

"Goblins are far too large for faeries to handle," murmured Jorran.

"But maybe not if several faeries work together," whispered Shellane.

The goblin campfire was almost out when the group arrived from the top of the forest. One of the goblins that had been hit with a club was lying in a pool of yellowish liquid that all considered to be goblin blood.

"That must be the one that lost the argument," quietly chuckled Jorran. The other four seemed to be asleep. The group landed in the underbrush away from the goblin camp, but where they could watch their movements while they thought of what to do. "I wish we had Orria here to tell us where she hid the clubs," complained Shellane.

"If we did, you couldn't handle them," answered Herman. "Remember what happened to Orria's hands."

"Then we need some kind of protection," enjoined Andron.

"Do you have any suggestions?" asked Herman.

"How about these thick leaves of this lacayo plant?" replied Shellane. "The plant would not mind giving its leaves for such a project."

"Great idea," said Herman. "Orria said you could lift them."

"Maybe we shouldn't have let Cheesey and Goossey go to the edge of the forest," Shellane suggested.

"If your report is correct, and I think it is, Jorran, this is the scouting party. The full army is waiting for their report."

Andron glowed, and suddenly went dim. "Then the main army is not expecting us. We can surprise them!" He was elated with his discovery.

"Then we let this group just keep scouting?" asked Herman.

"It's not a bad idea," Jorran theorized. "They will be confused when they can't find their clubs. Maybe they will even blame each other. They also may just keep on scouting. We will have to follow them and make sure they stay on the edge of the forest."

"But we don't know yet what Moussey found out," added Herman. "The goblin army may be on its way even now."

"We could scare this scouting party out of the forest." Shellane chuckled.

"You know, that is not a bad idea," said Herman.

"You're right," added Andron. "With their clubs gone, we could give them a brilliant blast of faerie light. I'm sure they have never seen it before. It ought to send them running."

"For how long?" asked Jorran, cautiously. "They are at least two days march into the forest. It would take them a while to get out."

"Not if they were running," muttered Shellane.

"You're right again, Shellane," exclaimed Herman, almost too loud. One of the goblins stirred. Everyone remained motionless.

"If we wait for them to finish their scouting, we will only prolong the inevitable," continued Shellane, gathering confidence in his ideas. "We will have to reveal ourselves sooner or later, especially if they start toward the center of the forest."

"This way we can get it over with, and be prepared as well," added Jorran.

"I don't want to fight, but we are going to have to some time," suggested Andron. "Why not at times of our choosing?"

"I wish we knew what Moussey had found out," said Herman quietly.

"We took Moussey's suggestion and placed people along the canopy," said Shellane.

"Yes! Let's see if he has been seen," added Andron.

"We can't sit and just wait," said Herman with conviction. The others knew he had made a decision. "We will wake these guys up, see what they do when they realize their clubs are gone, and at the same time send someone to the edge of the forest to get Moussey's report." All agreed. They made a lot of noise in the brush. The goblins awakened. Jorran's three companions were shocked at the language of these intruders spoke. They had to cover their ears when the goblins discovered the absence of their clubs. Then the goblins got worried. A discussion took place. Three of the goblins started to move down the trail in the direction they had come, back toward the forest edge and the goblin mountain. Then the leader spoke. They stopped; he motioned them back and pushed them roughly in the opposite direction, away from the edge of the forest. They complained loudly, but all walked on to continue their scouting, in spite of the darkness and the absence of their clubs.

Herman gave the signal, and Jorran rose to the canopy to send a messenger to the edge of the forest to get Moussey's report.

CHAPTER SIXTEEN

MOUSSEY'S DISCOVERY

Moussey began his search for the goblin mountain. He had flown only a short distance when he turned and saw Greena start off across the forest. As he saw her streak away, he suddenly remembered she had not renewed his supply of the dust.

"Well, this is a fine situation," he muttered to himself. "How long will the dust last now? I guess I had better get on with my plan."

He continued slowly, keeping the path in sight. He noticed that it got less black as he got farther away from the forest and closer to the foot of the mountains, yet the path remained easy to follow.

"I guess these guys leave a path of destruction anywhere they go," he thought to himself. "Nothing seems to like their feet on it."

The path, that was more like a scar on the earth, wound its way up the mountain, sometimes disappearing in thick forest or deep valleys.

Moussey kept himself high enough to be safe from discovery in case the goblin army, or another scouting team came from their mountain stronghold.

"I wish I could stay on the ground to search for this mountain. Maybe that will use up less dust," he murmured, almost afraid that he would be heard, even though he was many feet above the ground. "I wonder if the dust goes from us faster if we use it and slower if we don't use it." He hoped he would not have to find out that answer before there were others to help him.

The path came out of the more dense forest and became easier to follow. He continued following for about an hour through an open, almost treeless area, when he looked ahead and saw that it disappeared again into some trees. He rose above the trees and was faced with a huge, high cliff of solid exposed rock. He realized he had been so intent on watching the path that he was unaware of this mountain.

"Guess I'll have to walk a bit to see where this goes now," he muttered to himself.

He landed on the path. It was still cool. "The earth outside of the power of the dust probably can't heal as fast as in the forest," he muttered, and then suddenly closed his mouth, afraid that he might have been heard. He cautiously looked around for any advanced guards. Seeing none, he slowly walked under the trees.

The path went under the trees for about a mile. "This would be totally protected from anyone seeing it from above," he thought. "I guess the goblins aren't too stupid. They know how to put a path where it won't be discovered."

He also realized that the earth would heal itself and grow over the path, and then the way to the goblin mountain would be completely secret.

Suddenly, as he rounded a bend in the small forest, a huge opening, like a great gaping mouth, split the cliff in front of him. He knew he had found the entrance to the goblin mountain.

"Where are the guards?" he thought to himself, being very careful not to speak. He moved into the shadows of the trees, toward the gaping, black hole in the cliff face. It emitted a stench that almost made him throw up. "Get a hold on yourself, Moussey," he thought. "No time now to get weak and sick."

He waited at the mouth of the entrance until he got a little more used to the smell. "This is worse than the garbage dump at home. How do these people live in such a sickening place?" He answered his own question as he thought of the dead grass in the forest. "Goblins must possess a total disregard for the good things of the earth. How could they be expected to keep their home in a sanitary condition?"

He looked all about the opening, trying to discover a guard or sentry. He could see none. He thought it very curious and foolish that there was no one to watch for a stranger coming to this mountain stronghold. Then he realized, "They don't think anyone knows of them or that they are in the forest. I have caught them by surprise!" The thought elated Moussey. Then he got too curious and foolishly brave. He approached the mouth and noticed how much more bright he was; the dust was very brilliant in the darkness of this goblin "home." He noticed that he seemed even brighter than in normal darkness back above the forest at home. "These guys must live in a hole that is darker than night. How can they live in a place like this?" These thoughts were not enough to make him resist going further into the gaping maw.

His brilliance lit up the whole opening. It was huge. Even with the brilliance of the dust, he couldn't see the roof. He looked farther, deeper into the cave, for that is all he could call it. The darkness formed a black tunnel ahead of him. "I can't go into that. They will see me for miles with this dust glowing," he thought. "I guess it is time I got over my curiosity and went back to warn the others of the location of this place. Maybe there is something we can do to seal off the opening."

He walked back out into the light. He could not believe the difference, the warmth of the sun. "Boy are you stupid!" he said to himself. Suddenly realizing he had spoken aloud, he quickly regained the cover of the trees.

Then he heard a terrible sound. "Was it someone speaking?" he asked himself. The sound was coming from somewhere at the top of the opening. A short, ugly being, in Moussey's estimation anyway, standing on short, stubby legs, appeared at the top of the black hole.

He knew he had been heard, but he could not be seen at the moment. Would the brilliance of the dust betray him? The light was dim in the trees; surely this sentry would see him in the undergrowth lining the entrance.

Moussey got as close to the earth as he could. He tried to bury himself in it. He had never been so flat before. The guard looked around. He made some other sounds that Moussey assumed must be a language, but it was rough and hard on his ears. He had never heard anything so awful in his life. The sound frightened him so bad; he exerted all his self-control to resist getting up and trying to run away. He wondered how anything could make a sound so horrible.

The goblin held a club, a terrible looking weapon. "If one of us gets hit by that, we are goners," he thought. He even tried to keep his thoughts quiet. The goblin moved out of sight. "You better get out of here now," he thought, "even if he might be just hiding there." Moussey got up and ran away from the black entrance as fast as he could. All the pals were fast runners. Actually they were all very strong boys, in good physical condition and very well coordinated. He didn't know that the goblin had taken a trail to get to the bottom of the cliff, so he could take a closer look. If Moussey had not run when he did, he would have been discovered.

Moussey did not take time to look back. He had never wanted so much to get away from a place in his life. He ran until he had cleared the trees, then thought, "Fly!" He had not noticed, and could not have seen it anyway in the light of the day, how dim he had become. The dust was almost gone, fortunately. Otherwise he surely would have been discovered hiding in the underbrush at the black entrance. He rose only about ten feet off the ground. He did move somewhat faster than if he had been walking, but he knew this would not get him above all of the low trees and tall shrubs growing at the foot of the goblin mountain. He would have to fly around all of these things and that would take a lot of time. "Maybe I should save the dust for an emergency," he muttered, and then looked back fearfully to see if anyone had heard him.

As he concentrated, he heard the running of feet on the hard ground back in the tree-covered section of the path. He knew he must not be discovered. He exerted all the thought he could to the dust and rose into the air. He knew he would have to get high enough to be out of the vision of the running goblin. The power of his thought propelled him a hundred feet or so into the air. The goblin appeared at the edge of the trees, and stopped, suddenly feeling fearful of discovery. He did not look into the air; Moussey was safe for the time being, but he could feel himself slipping downward. The dust was fading.

The goblin slowly left the protection of the trees, one step at a time. Moussey got an idea. He moved himself above the goblin. If the dust faded completely, he wanted to be where he could use his weight to best advantage, falling on the guard. Moussey noticed that the goblin hid his eyes from the sun. "They must live in the dark all the time," he thought. "I must remember to tell the others of this weakness, if I get the chance."

He was now directly above the goblin. "Why wait for the dust to fade," he thought. "I can save the dust and drop on him from here." He suddenly dropped on the shoulders and head of the unsuspecting goblin. Moussey thought he had fallen on a piece of stone. The goblin went down, but Moussey's legs and buttocks were bruised from where he hit the goblin. The goblin was still conscious. His club had been knocked out of his hands; Moussey picked it up. It was quite heavy, but he could swing it. He thought for a split second that he might do terrible damage to the goblin if he hit him with this heavy thing, but immediately realized that worst damage would be done to him by the goblin if he got his club back. The goblin arose with his back to where Moussey had landed after the impact and as he turned around, Moussey swung, not as hard as he could; he didn't want to kill the goblin. "If I have to kill some goblins, it will have to be later," he thought, as he swung and connected with the head of the turning goblin. The goblin went down hard; Moussey approached cautiously to find out the damage he had done. The goblin looked up at him; surprise filled his eyes and then turned to terror. His head fell hard on the ground. Not knowing whether he had knocked him out or killed him, or if the goblin was faking, Moussey ran away, still holding the club. "This might come in handy," he thought as he ran down the path returning to the faerie forest, which was, as this moment, very far away.

As Moussey ran out of sight, the bewildered guard rose and staggered back into the protection of the trees, back to the entrance to the goblin mountain.

CHAPTER SEVENTEEN

GOBLIN COUNCIL

As Moussey ran away from the guard, he did not take the time to find out for sure what the guard did. When the goblin arose and ran back to the cover of the trees, he was frightened because he did not know what had happened to him. He had been told that the faeries were too small to be able to hurt him as he had just been hurt. He had to report this to his superiors in the mountain. Fortunately he did not turn back to see Moussey rise into the sky and fly off toward the forest. The goblin guard ran all the way to the entrance of the mountain and all the way down the tunnels to the center of his kingdom. His kingdom does not give off much light. Goblins do not like light. The Goblins kept the outside entrance to their world dark, to scare off intruders. It had worked for many, many years.

As the guard ran down the tunnel, others heard his footsteps. This is what happened, in our own language, so we can understand it. There were many to welcome him. In his own, not attractive language, he told those that met him of the strange experience that had just befallen him.

"You are not telling the truth, Laguck. Ain't no one who can hurt us like this. No one would dare."

"Is the truth," exclaimed Laguck. "What would I git for lyin'?"

The leader of this group took him to a higher authority.

"You lie, Laguck!" he was told. No one could believe that this could happen. He finally came to the king of the goblins himself. The king lived in the deepest part of the mountain stronghold. He hated the light more than anyone. His was the dimmest part of the goblin world. He was very concerned when he heard the story of the young guard. But he was no fool. He knew that the guard had been sleeping or he would have seen the intruder before he got to the entrance to the mountain.

"You shall spend several months in prison for your laziness," commanded the king.

The guard was placed in prison for his delinquent acts while on guard duty. The king tried to make an example of the young guard, but he knew that his people were lazy, slothful, and uncaring about their neighbor or anyone else and he, the king, was the most uncaring in the kingdom. But he knew the goblins could be stirred up to jealousy. The greedy king wanted what he had once seen the faeries carrying many years ago. He remembered how he had first seen the little people.

Long ago, the faeries had come out of their forest for a foolish reason. Two faeries, who wanted what the outside world could give, had convinced the faerie king to venture out of the confining protection, as they called it, of the faerie forest. This had never been done before. They had led the faerie king to believe he could have influence in the outside world. In order to truly exercise his influence, he must be on the ground, not in flight. The faerie king paraded his finery at the edge of the forest, but saw no one from the outer world. Wisdom replaced foolishness and he guided his people back into the protective cover of their forest, but not before his folly had been discovered by the future goblin king. The two discontented faeries accompanied the king back into the forest, but finally deserted the faerie kingdom and flew off into the outer world.

The future goblin king remembered seeing these beautiful people, so much smaller than he, walking into the forest with fine clothes and many pretty things hanging about their necks. He especially noticed the king and queen of the faeries. He vowed he would one day possess the beautiful things that they carried. He knew there must be great riches in that forest. The future king of the goblins had not seen the faeries rise into the air because he had turned away to escape the bright sun. He had seen them go into the forest, however, so he knew where they lived. He also knew that the only way he would ever get all these riches would be to become king. He had worked all his life to accomplish this and had stirred up the goblins to go fight the faeries and get all the riches they had.

The king remembered the nights when he had quietly left the protection of the mountain cavern and scouted the faerie forest. He remembered with joyous hatred seeing the first glowing creature walking on the trail at the edge of the forest.

"It's one of them cursed creatures," he had thought to himself. "I wonder how they makes themselves glow."

He recalled hiding along the trail the next night, and not seeing the creature again. He recalled the third night creeping up on the unsuspecting creature and bashing it with his club.

"They is tiny and no match for my club," he had said to himself in triumph.

He recalled returning each night for three more nights, and not seeing any of the creatures. Then on the fourth night after the murder, another had been walking on the ground. He recalled sneaking up on the creature and bashing it with his club.

Three more nights passed with no creatures, and then two of them. The same result. He was sure of success if they came against him in battle.

"So they glows," he had said to himself. "They is too small to hurt us."

He then found ten trusted goblins to come with him, so he could show them the puny creatures and plan how to destroy them. But he never saw another one, even though his scouting party came out each night to find them. Finally he gave up his scouting the edge of the faerie forest, but he continued to think about how he would enter and attack the forest itself.

The future goblin king had not known that the king of the faeries had caught a glimpse of him when he saw the faeries parading in their finery. The faerie king had not let anyone know what he had seen. Unsure of what he had seen, he sent brave scouts to the edge of the forest to keep watch. When the first one did not report in, he looked for him and found the body. He sent the second one, unfortunately, with the same result. Then he sent two, hoping they would be able, together, to successfully fight off the enemy who was murdering his people. After the deaths of the final two, he sent more scouts, but instructed them to stay out of sight in the thick foliage of the trees. It was this scouting party that saw the goblin king come with his trusted ten goblins. The faerie king swore his scouts to secrecy, and began the plans to protect his kingdom against these terrible foes. These first scouts consisted of Andron, Shandra, and Jorran. When he was ready, he included the queen and others in the group, and held a council in the Council Clearing. He invited the elders of the kingdom to join them, hoping they might know something of these terrible murderous creatures. As he described to the elders what he had seen the day he foolishly paraded outside of the forest, the oldest of the elders became very frightened.

"I have not heard of these creatures for years almost beyond memory. My father told me of them. They are terrible. He called them Goblins. He would tell me no more." After hearing this, the council decided to search for someone who could help them.

Because the faerie king kept his faeries out of sight after the murders, the future goblin king had no real idea who or what he was fighting. He knew his goblins were strong, mean, and able to win any fight they got into. They had been stealing food from the mountain people for hundreds of years, and never been caught, at least no one ever lived to tell of it. The big people of the mountains were afraid of the night at certain times of the year and some of them even put out the food so the people of the night, as the goblins were known to them, would not bother them. The goblins had a huge cache of food in the darkest part of their world. They didn't need to go out and attack anybody very often, but they did it just to see what they could get. If the food went bad, it didn't make any difference. The smell of rotting food was part of the stench that almost made Moussey throw up. Rotting food is not a very good source of nourishment, but it is all they could get when they refused to raise anything themselves. If they attacked too much, then the big people would unite and fight. When that happened, the goblins always lost. No big people had seen the goblins for many years.

The goblin king knew he must give his fellow goblins a good reason to attack the faeries. He thought about the report of the guard as he told of Moussey's attack. "I think I knows of a way I can make the goblins mad, so's they will fight," the king thought to himself.

He got his goblins together and said, "We been openly attacked by many of them creatures. How else could they beat one of our goblins? These creatures ain't that big. They is cowards. Was no reason for this attack. What we goin' to do about it? Are we gonna to sit back and do nothin'?"

"No!" cried the goblins. "We must attack!"

"But the scouts ain't back," argued the king. "Maybe we should wait for 'em?"

"They probably kilt them too!" shouted one very large and extra ugly goblin.

"Maybe we should go find out," said another.

"I don't know," said the king. "We'd have to fight extra hard cause we don't know where they is, or what kind of weapons they got."

"I say we find out by bashin' in their heads!" roared the large ugly one.

"It's true they come to our home and attacked us," said the king with a wicked grin. "Things like that don't deserve to live. Maybe we ought to go get 'em so's they don't come and attack us no more. They might have some treasure that we can git too."

"Yeah," said another. "You told us about lots o' pretty things they got."

"They gots things we deserve to have. How come they have all the nice things and we only gits this little hole in the mountain?" asked the king.

Their mountain home was actually very large; they had just been too lazy to investigate all of it.

"I hates them that has more than we have!" yelled another.

"Yeah!" roared the whole group.

"What we goin' to do about it?" yelled the king.

"Let's go get 'em and bash 'em!" yelled another.

"Yeah!" yelled the whole group.

"When we start?" cried a goblin standing by the big ugly one.

"The sooner the better!" yelled the big ugly one. His name was Shulkgak.

"Shulkgak has spoke for all of us," cried another.

"Back to your nests and grab what food you can and let's get goin!" yelled the king over the yells and cries of the goblins.

"Everyone take two clubs," said another, whose name was Gillguk.

By the time all the goblins returned with their clubs and food supplies, most of the night had passed. "I been out to the mountain entrance," said Shulkgak. "That cursed sun will come up soon. I hates to go out in the sun."

The king was so anxious to get going to the war that he would go out even in the light of day, which he hated and knew all goblins hated and feared. His goblins would be braver in the dark. So he decided to wait. "We waits until almost dark, then we moves. Everyone to the entrance. We waits there. Go get some of the fire drink we stole from the big people," the king said to the small wicked goblin, whose name was Gackix. Take help with you and bring lots. We need to keep ourselves fired up for this war while we waits for the dark." Gackix smiled a wicked smile of understanding and pointed to several of the hoard who went with him to get the fire drink.

CHAPTER EIGHTEEN

MOUSSEY'S CHALLENGE

Moussey hoped he had not killed the goblin. "Maybe I'd better go back and see if he is all right," he thought to himself. He dropped to the ground and ran back to the turn in the trail and peeked around a bush and saw that the goblin was no longer where he had fallen. Moussey looked at the club.

"If this hits a faerie, they are dead," he moaned to himself. "Then why am I so upset if I might have hurt that goblin? He would have killed me without a thought."

"I have to warn somebody about this."

"Do I run or fly? The dust is fading fast. Will it fade slower if I don't use it?" He decided to save the dust, hoping it would not fade as fast if he didn't use it. As he ran along the trail, he became aware of the difficulty facing him. The trail first descended into a deep valley, then started up the other side. It became very steep and Moussey discovered he was very tired and the club was becoming very heavy. He suddenly realized he was hungry.

"How did we ever expect to run an army without any food?" He came to the conclusion that all of them had gotten carried away with the excitement of the moment when they discovered the goblin trail in the forest. He looked at the sun. It was already early evening.

"Not much daylight left. If I fly and lose the dust, I'll be grounded. If they come looking for me, I may need the dust to let them see me, if there is enough left to produce any kind of light." The steep trail made Moussey's hunger very acute; he was becoming weak. He concentrated all his energies in getting to the top of the trail. When he arrived, huffing and puffing, the trail greeted him with another valley, even deeper than the one he had just crossed. The trail disappeared into the trees, winding down, down, deep into the now dark floor of the valley.

"I didn't notice all the valleys and hills when I was flying." he muttered to himself.

Moussey decided in desperation to fly across. He slowly rose into the sky as he exerted all his power of thought to make the dust work. He rose about ten feet into the air.

"Not even high enough to clear the trees." He knew now that he must save the dust to make himself visible to someone looking for him. "Hope they look for me tonight so they can see my dust. I'm sure I haven't enough to glow in the daylight. If I can't fly, then I had better see if this forest has any food to offer me."

He began looking along the trail for any berries or fruits. He noticed that the other side of this valley was much higher than where he was standing. "If I can get to the other side, maybe I'll be in a better position to be seen, if someone comes looking for me." He decided to push himself one more time and ran down to the floor of the valley. It was not totally dark on the floor of the valley but the shadows were deep and getting deeper every step he took. They played tricks on his mind, making him see things that were not really there.

"No time to get scared, Moussey. Just keep running." He was so weak from hunger that he could only stumble up the other side of the valley. The setting sun greeted his arrival at the top of the valley. He was glad to see even the twilight of the setting sun, but then noticed that the trail went even higher.

"I must find some food before the sun goes down." He slowly continued up the trail, searching each side for some sign of food bearing vegetation. Just as the last light of the sun faded, he noticed something red off the trail a little ways. He staggered through the underbrush and was rewarded with a fine patch of wild raspberries. They were ripe and delicious. They helped his thirst as well as his hunger. It was totally dark when he finished his simple dinner.

"I must keep going. The closer I am to the faerie forest when I am found, the better. Hope I can stay on the trail in the dark." Moussey had never been in such a dark place in his life. He had to move slowly so he didn't wander off the trail. He could hear many sounds in the underbrush. He exerted all his power of thought to ignore the sounds of the night creatures moving in the forest. The trail rose steadily upward, becoming more and more steep with every step.

"I must get to the top of this mountain. No one will ever see me down in this dark valley." Moussey was sweating and cold. The jacket that he carried was not heavy enough to keep him warm on the high slopes of the mountain. Each step was becoming a major effort. The light refreshment of the raspberries was quickly wearing off. He was hunched over, clawing at the trail with his hands to keep himself going forward. Then his feet slipped and he fell on his face, his breath coming in short gasps. He lay for a while to gather his energy. A sudden sound at the side of the trail brought him to his senses. He ran frantically up the trail. The trail suddenly turned to his right and a dim light greeted him, shining through the thick trees. He ran to the light, which became brighter and brighter. He noticed that the trees were becoming less and less dense. The light had a soft blue glow to it. He laughed out loud as he emerged into a meadow at the top of the mountain trail. A full moon greeted his weary eyes. Never had the moon been so bright and warm and comforting.

He staggered out into the meadow, hoping he would be seen more easily there than in the shadow of the trees. The fearful scurrying of the night creatures was not as loud away from the trees. He decided to take a short nap under the warm blanket of the full moon. Moussey found a soft patch of grass. He was asleep as soon as his head touched the ground. Anyone passing overhead would have noticed, if they were looking for it, a dim glow in the middle of the meadow. Moussey had exerted all the energy left in him to give one last thought to the faerie dust before falling into a deep sleep.

CHAPTER NINETEEN

THE FAERIE ARMY MOVES

Herman and Shellane watched the goblin scouting party until it disappeared into the forest. They then slowly rose to the canopy of the forest, where the rest of the faeries were awaiting any news from the faerie scout sent to the edge of the forest to find Moussey. Herman assigned two faeries to stay with the goblin scouting party, following them from high in the protecting limbs of the trees. "Every hour, one of you rise to the canopy and get your bearings so you always know where you have to go to get any messages to us." Herman wanted all the faeries to keep someone in sight. He could take no chances that anything would happen without some help being immediately available.

He then turned to one of the other faeries. "I know that the king returned to the center of the kingdom to get the army ready. Go to him and ask him to come with the full army to the edge of the forest. We will be waiting for him there.

"If the goblins are near the edge of the forest," said Shellane thoughtfully.

"We have to assume that they might be," added Shandra, who had been impatiently waiting at the canopy.

"Shandra is right. Tell the king to have the faerie army stay as dim as possible. They will not be able to move as fast, but they must come as quickly as they can." Herman felt very old; he had never had such a responsibility in his life. "To move such an army may take most of the day," said Andron. "Large groups of faeries cannot move as fast as smaller groups. Some may be crossing the forest as the night falls."

Herman gave some further orders to another faerie. "Fly to all of the faeries assigned to be the guides across the forest. Tell them to rise high in the sky so the advancing army can see them and use them as a point of focus in order to move faster. We must be ready by this evening to move on any advice that Moussey has discovered."

The faerie streaked away. "How can she know where she is going?" asked Shellane.

"She has many of the points memorized," answered Shandra. "We have been practicing while you were playing with the goblins down on the forest floor."

"We must get to the edge of the forest and set up places for the army to take its stand," said Herman, ignoring Shandra's attempt at humor. "I'm glad you have been practicing. Take us as quickly as you can to the place where the trail enters the forest."

They all focused on Shandra and Andron, and in the power of their dust, became golden streaks of light, starting their crossing of the great forest, from one checkpoint faerie to another.

"The young faerie did well," commented Shellane, a little surprised. "She has already gotten the message to the guide faeries to be up in the sky as they see us coming."

"I hope that our enthusiasm stays as strong when we see the actual goblin army, wherever it is and whenever it comes," replied Herman.

Herman noted by his watch that it took five minutes for the small party of faeries to cross the forest. He was amazed at the vast expanse of this forest. "How can the goblins ever find you in this huge forest?" he asked Shandra.

"We are afraid of what they might do to the forest while they are trying to find us and if their army is large enough, and they get going in the right direction, they might eventually find their way to the center of the kingdom."

"That is a chance we cannot take," said Andron. "That is why you were found. We must stop them at the edge, before they ever get in."

"They might scar the forest beyond repair," said another young faerie, who had joined them as they arrived at the edge of the forest. "Greena told me how the forest can repair itself, but how much can it take?"

"I hope we don't have to find out," answered Herman, quietly. "Where are Cheesey and Goossey?"

The faeries looked at each other. "Someone has to tell him," exclaimed Jorran turning to face Herman. "They went down the trail to find Moussey. We told them they should stay and wait for you."

"But they just said that they had to find out what had happened to their buddy," added Ewanille, a beautiful young girl with long golden hair, that glowed magnificently, even in the early morning light.

"Then we have no word from Moussey yet?" asked Herman.

"None," replied Jorran.

"How long have they been gone?"

"About two hours," replied Falslevia. "They left before the daylight. We gave them another shot of the dust."

"But what if they are too bright!" said Herman, impatiently.

"They have been working on dimming themselves all night," replied Ewanille.

"They actually do quite well," encouraged Jorran, seeing Herman's concern.

"Two faeries went with them," said another faerie sitting near Herman, as all were now on the ground, just inside the edge of the forest, in the safety of the dense trees.

Herman looked at the faerie. "My name is Needlesetheria," said the young boy faerie, somewhat shyly. "It is quite a mouthful, I know."

"We call him Needles for short," said Shandra with a grin. Needles had short, dark brown, curly hair and was all dress in green except for his bright yellow hat.

Herman started to notice that age was not a determining factor as to whether a faerie was in the army or not. "You are quite young aren't you, Needles?" he asked.

"By faerie reckoning, I guess," he politely answered. "But I am one of the fastest in the kingdom." He beamed with great pride.

"It's true," said Shellane with a grin similar to Shandra's. "He has an uncanny ability to miss things as he flies through the forest, as well as keep track of where he is and where he has been."

Herman smiled as he noted the proud carriage of this young faerie. Looking around he noticed that some faeries were missing. "Where are Greena and Orria? They came here with Cheesey and Goossey didn't they?"

Jorran looked at the others. "They went with Cheesey and Goossey," answered Needles, courageously.

"I guess it had to be," said Herman. "There is no way to protect any of us, is there?"

All shook their heads. "Okay," cried Herman, startling everyone into readiness for action. "Let's get the strategic points established for the army when it gets here. You've all been fading with fear and sorrow. No one is hurt yet."

The faeries suddenly glowed so brightly that Herman had to remind them to stay under control.

"We need a war council," said Ewanille.

Plans were then carefully conceived to place the army along the edge of the forest, not too spread out, and with greater parts deeper into the forest, so the goblins would think they had won, if they broke through the first barrier of faeries. Leaves were prepared to protect the faeries' hands when they handled the clubs. They were to take the clubs into the air and drop them on the goblins' heads, hopefully knocking them out of action.

"What about the brilliance of the dust?" suggested Ewanille. "I can be very bright with all this hair, if I need to be."

"She is right," added Jorran. "Her hair can be like a small star in the sky."

"We must keep the brilliance of the dust as a last resort," responded Herman. "We don't know if the goblins will have some protection from it."

"They don't know about it," said Falslevia.

"Are you sure, absolutely sure?" asked Andron.

"I guess we are really not sure about anything," said Needles, thoughtfully.

"We have a saying in my country," said Herman with a smile. "We will just have to play it by ear." The faeries all looked at each other, touching their ears. "I mean we will have to wait and see, and if we think it is worth trying, well, we'll try it."

"Oh," said the faeries together, still not sure what Herman's country did with their ears.

A faerie suddenly dropped from the canopy. "The front of the army is at the last guide point," she said. "They'll be here any minute!"

All followed her to the canopy to greet the king and the army, ready to make final preparations for what was to come. "I wish my buddies and Orria and Greena would get back here." Herman thought to himself. "It's great to get ready, but what are we getting ready for?" The arrival of the king of the faeries and the first vanguard of the army brought Herman out of his thoughts. "Greetings, Your Majesty. Let's get your army organized along the edge of the forest, ready for whatever is going to come."

"I wish I knew what that was, Herman," said the king.

"I share your wishes, sire," answered the young general of the army of the faeries.

CHAPTER TWENTY

Moussey Is Found

Upon their arrival at the edge of the faerie forest, Goossey and Cheesey looked with great anticipation for their comrade. Moussey was nowhere in sight. "I thought he would be here by now!" exclaimed Cheesey.

"Greena said she didn't get the chance to give him another shot of the dust. He could be walking down the trail in the dark and we wouldn't be able to see him," responded Goossey.

"But he would be able to see us," answered his comrade with some enthusiasm.

"Right. So now what do we do?"

There were faeries all along the edge of the forest. "Do we know where the trail is?" asked Goossey anxiously.

"Yes," answered one. "Over there." She pointed to a path that led away from the forest. "Greena described it to us, and that is the only path that leads away from the forest."

"It must be it," muttered Cheesey, almost afraid that there were goblins that would hear his voice. A faerie was suspended in the air over the trail, guarding it.

"Well, let's get on down the trail," suggested Goossey.

"Herman told us that no one was to go down the trail until he arrived here," said the faerie lighting the trail.

"It is too dark," said Cheesey to his comrade. "We had better wait until dawn at least."

"Yeah, let's wait until morning," agreed Goossey. The two friends moved off by themselves as if they were going to find a place to sleep.

"We've got to get down that trail," whispered Goossey.

"I know," answered his friend. "But it is too dark to do much good. Maybe we'd better wait until it starts to get light."

"Greena and Orria came here with us. They went to check on the faeries guarding the edge of the forest. They would light the way so we wouldn't need the morning light," muttered Goossey.

"We'll have to wait until they return," whispered his pal. "We need them to keep us supplied with the dust."

"And recharge Moussey when we find him," added Goossey.

The two pals looked off in the direction of the trail, hoping that their missing pal was all right. Sleep overcame their worry.

Suddenly Orria and Greena appeared at their sides. "The trail guard told us you had come off this way," said Orria. "What are you doing?"

"Don't you think we should get looking for Moussey?" added Greena.

"We thought we should wait for the morning," said Cheesey, without much conviction.

"It will be morning in a short time," said Orria. "Let's get going."

"But the guard said she had orders from Herman that we should wait for him," whispered Goossey, also without much conviction.

"Then let's sneak past the guard," said Cheesey thoughtfully. "We can rise high in the sky and she won't see us."

"Faeries are used to other faerie light," corrected Greena.

"Yes, she would know what we were doing," added Orria. "Why don't we just go tell her that we are going. What is she going to do to stop us?"

The pals looked at each other and then at the eager faerie friends. "We have got to find Moussey," whispered Goossey with such enthusiasm that the others shushed him.

They all rose into the sky. "It won't be light for a while, but we can light the way with the dust," said Orria.

As they moved toward the trail, the guard faerie moved in front of them. "What are you doing?" she asked.

"Going to look for our pal," said Goossey with authority. "Tell Herman we will find him."

"We can't wait any longer," added Greena pleadingly. "I was the one that let him go without any dust or food. I was supposed to come back to find him. I didn't make it. I have to find him!" "Please tell Herman what we are doing," said Cheesey. "He will understand."

"Do you have a sufficient supply of the dust?" The guard was looking at Cheesey and Goossey. "If you are going down the trail toward the goblins, you better not take the risk of running out."

The two pals thanked the wise young faerie and received an extra supply of dust from Orria and Greena.

The guard moved aside and the four comrades slowly flew off, finally disappearing around a bend in the trail.

"Flying together or walking together, we are very bright. We will be seen for miles in the dark," commented Greena. "We need a plan of search and we must separate to cover more territory and be less obvious to anyone coming down the trail."

"But that someone might be Moussey." All understood the concern in Goossey's voice. They all knew that it was almost inevitable that Moussey would be grounded by now. Surely the dust could not last this long on a big person.

"We may have to take the chance of being seen in order to find Moussey," said Cheesey.

"Let's spread out along the trail," instructed Orria. "Three of us stay together to light the trail so we can see Moussey in the dark, and one of us fly ahead to watch for the army of goblins."

"Great idea," agreed the others.

"I'll fly ahead," said Orria. "You big guys are like some of the big bright signs we've seen in your world. If Moussey is walking, he will be on the trail and we will see him."

"If he is lost in the trees by the trail, he'll be able to see us," encouraged Greena.

"Or if he's not near any of the trail . . ." Cheesey did not finish the thought.

"We must be more positive than that," scolded Orria. "Let's stop planning and get looking." All agreed and the search began.

"We can move fairly fast," said Goossey. "We light up the trail for quite a distance."

The group moved quickly along the trail, Orria well ahead to watch for the goblin army.

The trail ran flat and straight for some distance, then began a steep climb. "I'm glad I'm flying," commented Goossey. "That trail would be tiring to walk on."

"Moussey will probably be walking on it, and he hasn't eaten all day," added Greena.

"He hasn't eaten since we left our forest back home where we first met you," added Cheesey. The friends moved up the trail a little faster.

The trail slowly rose higher and higher toward the mountains. The friends had searched for about an hour when Orria suddenly appeared beside them. "How did you know where to find us?" asked Cheesey.

"You can be seen for miles from up in the sky," answered Orria with a grin. "There is a wide meadow up ahead. I didn't want to go into it without all of us being together. The army could be in it. Moussey could be in it. We will have to spread out and search across it."

"Lead on, Macduff," said Cheesey enthusiastically.

""My name is not Macduff," said Orria, totally bewildered by Cheesey's comment.

"Just a saying by my people," said Cheesey.

"We'd better get high so we fly there faster," continued Cheesey, smiling at Orria's still bewildered face.

"No need to. I have a picture of the place." All concentrated on Orria and they streaked to the edge of the meadow. It was very long and wide.

"We can't cover this whole thing in one pass. We'll have to break it down in sections," instructed Greena.

"Right," agreed Cheesey. "And if Moussey is in the trees, he'll be able to see us as we fly across." The detailed search of the meadow began.

The friends did not know that Moussey would not be watching for them. He was exhausted and sleeping near one edge of the meadow.

"The morning is not far off," commented Orria. The sky was just beginning to show the first signs of dawn. "We must finish this search before the dawn, or we will be totally exposed to friend or foe."

"Surely they can see us now if they are hiding in the trees," said Goossey with a grin. "We must look like a small star, all of us here together."

"I guess you're right," answered Orria as the friends started their first flight across the meadow.

Cheesey flew next to the trees surrounding the meadow, Orria next to him, then Goossey and then Greena. They flew about twenty feet apart. Suddenly Greena squealed with delight. "I see him." The others saw her drop to the ground and were immediately at her side. Moussey was sleeping very soundly in the grass. The friends noticed that his clothing was dirty and torn at the knees. His hands were covered with caked dirt as well as his face, except for where sweat had run down to make little lines down his cheeks. The group was not prepared for the sight. Tears ran down their cheeks.

"Okay," said Goossey, wiping the tears away. "Do we wake him up, or wait for him to wake up?"

"We have to awaken him," answered Greena. "We will be exposed in a very short time by the dawn. We must get into the protection of the trees."

Goossey put his hand gently on Moussey's shoulder and gave it a gentle shake. "I don't want to scare him."

"No time to worry about that," Orria corrected. "We've got to get out of this meadow."

Goossey shook harder. Moussey stirred. "Shake him again," cried Greena.

Goossey made sure Moussey awakened with the next shake. Moussey rolled on his back and slowly opened his eyes. He could not believe what he saw at first. Then tears came to his eyes. "I had almost given up hope of being found. If I hadn't found this meadow when I did, you may have never found me. Am I as dirty as I feel?"

"You are the greatest sight I have ever seen," answered his pal Cheesey.

Greena took charge as she gave him a supply of dust. "We must get him to the protection of the trees. Orria, go find some water so we can get him cleaned up."

The four friends slowly flew to the protection of the trees while Orria looked for water. "Here," she called from another side of the meadow. The group moved instantly to her side.

She had found a little clear brook with a small pond in the middle. "A perfect place for a bath," said Cheesey with a laugh. "But probably a little cool."

Moussey didn't wait. He went to the edge and dipped in his hands and splashed the cool water on his face. It was very refreshing and he felt better immediately. "Better not get too wet," commented Orria. "The dawn will be quite cold."

"I don't suppose anyone brought any food," asked Moussey with anticipation. The tears returned as the friends opened their knapsacks and gave the very hungry comrade some food and smiled as they watched him devour it. Then they all sat down and ate their breakfast and prepared themselves to hear Moussey's report.

CHAPTER TWENTY-ONE

PREPARATIONS FOR THE BATTLE

As the friends listened to Moussey's report, it became evident that some quick decisions had to be made. Was the goblin army ready to march? When would it come? They knew it had not come yet. They were in the middle of the trail, halfway between the goblin mountain and the faerie forest. Moussey assured them that there was no other way. They finally decided that someone needed to go back and give Herman the report, and the rest needed to go to the goblin mountain to be there when the army immerged. Then they could fly and have the faerie army well prepared before the goblins arrived. They may even be able to set some traps along the trail.

It was finally decided that Orria was to return to the forest and report. The others would follow the trail both ways, back to the mountain and back to the faerie forest to see where some traps could be set. Moussey and Greena went the direction of the mountain and Cheesey and Goossey went toward the faerie forest. Orria was to return and find Goossey and Cheesey so she could make sure they had a constant supply of the dust. Greena and Orria gave the pals another supply of the dust before Orria left. Having to concentrate on making lots of light on the trail at night had used up a great deal of the supply the pals had.

"You realize that the supply of the dust on us lasts longer if we don't have to use it so much. The more we concentrate, the more it goes." All agreed with Moussey.

"You still had a little glow about you when I found you," said Orria. "How did you do it?"

"I walked all the way," answered Moussey. "There was not enough dust to get me over the trees, so I saved it. Just before I went to sleep, I concentrated hard on being bright. I guess the dust maintained the thought."

"We are really discovering many things about this stuff," commented Cheesey.

"We'd better get going," said Goossey.

"They hate the sun." Moussey remembered how the goblin had not liked to come out of the protection of the trees. "Hopefully that means they won't march until it is darker."

"Depends on how desperate they are, and how bad they want to fight," responded Goossey.

"That is an important point to consider anyway. Herman should know about it," said Orria. "I'll be back soon. I can picture the forest so I'll be there quickly. You two going back to the mountain, be careful and don't be heroic or foolish."

"Yeah," added Goossey, "remember you are only scouting."

"As soon as we get to the mountain, we'll send back a report," yelled Moussey as he and Greena flew off into the trees.

Orria streaked away to make her report.

"Let's get with it," counseled Goossey. The two pals flew slowly, following the trail back toward the faerie forest, looking for good places to set ambushes.

Orria returned with Herman, Falslevia, Needles, and Jorran. Shortly after Herman met Goossey and Cheesey, Greena arrived and informed them that the goblins had not left the mountain, but that she and Moussey had heard them yelling and talking in their hideous language just inside the entrance to the mountain. "Moussey doesn't think they will leave until it is dark, or at least until the sun is not so bright," she informed the group.

"We can't take any chances," said Herman. "We must continue to scout the trail to find places to ambush the goblins. They are too big to fight hand to hand. We must find ways to throw them off guard, surprise them. I'm convinced it's the only way we can defeat them. Greena, take me to the mountain. Jorran. You, Needles, and Falslevia scout the trail between here and the mountain for places of ambush. The rest of you continue toward the forest and do the same. Let's go."

Everyone flew off in his or her respective directions. Goossey, Cheesey, and Orria found five good places for ambush, blind turns in the trail, steep parts of the trail, and places where the trail was very narrow. Orria flew to the forest to inform Andron, whom Herman had put in charge of the army in his absence. Andron flew back with Orria and inspected each of the places indicated by the friends. They then sat down and thought of ways that they could use the places to their best advantage.

"I think we should place one of us at the turns in the trail," suggested Goossey. "There are two of them. As they make the turn, faeries could give them a bright blast of dust light and we could rush in and take their clubs and throw them into the brush at the sides of the trail. Then other faeries could come and lift them with the dust and take them away. Moussey said they didn't like the sun. They live in a dark cave. Imagine how bright a blast of dust light would be in total darkness."

"I don't know how many we can get with that method," said Jorran, a little doubtful.

"Neither do I," responded Goossey. "But if we can't fight them hand to hand, then we will have to take them a little at a time."

"It's too bad we don't know the size of the army," commented Orria.

"I guess you're right," said Jorran, thoughtfully. "Could we set both of you up at the first turn, then have you move to the next one to do the same thing?"

"If we do it only twice, they shouldn't have time to think we'll do it again," answered Cheesey.

"There is a narrow place in between," said Orria. "What will we do there?"

"We could blind them with the dust and drop the clubs on them we collected the first time," suggested Cheesey. "And Goossey and I could hit them from the bushes."

"What if they hit you?" asked Orria.

"We all have to take chances," said Goossey, not with much confidence.

"Our defense is based on the fact that they will be temporarily blinded by the dust," said Jorran. "What if they are not blinded, or even affected by the dust?"

No one had an answer.

"Hey, look! It's Moussey and Greena," cried Goossey.

"How ya doin', guys," said Moussey as he landed gently on the ground.

"How are your plans coming?" asked Greena.

"Herman sent us here to compare plans," answered Moussey. "We found some narrow sections of the trail and some steep parts where we might be able to roll things down on them."

"All we have to do is find something to roll," said Greena with a grin.

"How much dust would it take to lift a large rock and place it to be rolled?" asked Cheesey. Everyone looked at each other.

"Not a bad idea," cried Jorran with delight. "Let's find out." They all took to the air and flew to a rocky place higher on the mountain, but far from the goblin cave. The faeries supplied the dust. A huge rock was completely covered. Cheesey tried to lift it.

"I can move it," he cried. "But I can't lift it yet."

"Let me help." Goossey joined him in the lift. Up the rock came.

"But can we move it through the air?" asked Moussey doubtfully.

"Let's try and fly with it," groaned Goossey.

He and Cheesey got barely off the ground. "Give it some more dust!" cried Orria. She and Andron rose above the rock and gave an additional, large supply. The rock rose into the air.

"We can lift it!" yelled Cheesey with delight.

"Move it to the place where we need it," directed Moussey. "Follow me. The rest of you get some more."

Andron, Orria, and Greena supplied more dust on another rock, not quite as big as the first one. Then the three faeries tried to lift it. "Need more dust," Greena cried. The three faeries gave another ample supply.

Suddenly Orria drifted to the ground. She looked very bewildered. The rock fell to the ground and all rushed over to her. Moussey and the pals arrived and got to her first as the faeries could not move fast. "What is going on?" asked Andron. "I can hardly get myself into the air." Greena expressed the same problem.

"You used too much of your personal dust supply on the rocks," said Moussey. "They were very big. It took a lot of dust for us to be able to lift them."

The faeries were completely unaware that this could happen. "We have never needed to give so much dust before," said Andron, looking at the other two faeries.

"But what do we do now?" asked Goossey. "Can you fly at all?"

"Will the dust return?" asked Cheesey.

"Can you three lift the second rock?" asked Andron, taking charge of a difficult situation. The three pals found they could and flew off to the steep trail where they had placed the other rock and returned to the three faeries. The three weakened faeries were in serious conversation.

"We must inform the king," said Greena.

"One of you will have to go," said Orria to the pals. "We can't fly fast enough."

"Go while you have the dust on you," urged Andron. "We can't give you any more." Cheesey rose into the air and streaked away. A quiet group of friends sat on the rocky ground.

"We should have told Cheesey to bring many more faeries to help lift more rocks," counseled Greena.

"We can't continue to risk your ability to fly to get more rocks," said Moussey with concern.

"We have to stop the goblins," said Orria with conviction. "We can't let them get to our forest." Just then Cheesey arrived with about fifty faeries including the king, Shandra, and Shellane.

"I brought some reinforcements," said Cheesey proudly. The king directed the other faeries to dust some more rocks.

"How many will we need?" he asked. The pals were amazed at the sacrifice of the faeries. "We must stop the goblins at any cost," the king pointed out as he saw the concern in the pal's eyes.

"Will these faeries fly again?" asked Goossey.

"Hopefully with some rest," said the king.

The pals moved two more huge boulders; there wasn't room for any more. Suddenly Orria sat up and yelled. "Herman must know of this." She tried to rise, but moved still quite slowly. "Moussey, you know the way," she said imploringly.

"I don't have the picture in mind. I won't fly too fast."

"You must go immediately," said the king. He pointed to two faeries to go with Moussey. "We can't have you running out of dust." Moussey rose and flew off over the forest toward the goblin mountain. "Move everyone to the meadow," commanded the king. Lifting the three weak faeries, they all flew to the meadow.

"Why aren't the other faeries tired?" asked Cheesey.

"They shared the distribution of the dust on the rocks. No one used too much," answered the king. "Now we must get these three back to the forest."

"We don't want to miss the battle," cried Greena.

"We've worked too long and hard," said Orria.

"Hopefully you will be all right in a short time," said the king. "But you must get some food and rest." They were again lifted by their comrades and with the speed of the dust flew to the faerie forest.

The king sent Shellane and Shandra to organize ambushes. Many faeries went with them. "We must be ready well before night fall. We don't know when the goblins will come."

A large group of faeries arrived with a supply of lacoya leaves to protect their delicate hands when they would have to touch the clubs. The pals guided them to the places where the ambushes would take place. The leaves were placed in the underbrush along the two sections of the trail. Herman and Falslevia suddenly arrived. "Problems, Your Majesty?"

"I think we should move half of the army to the ambush places to handle the clubs and produce the light of the dust," suggested the king.

Herman thought a moment. "You're right, sire. The battle will be fought here, outside of your forest and far from it. Tell me of your preparations."

After hearing from the king and giving approval to the plans and sending Shellane and Shandra to return and spread half of the faerie army along the trail, Herman talked to the king about what could be done to start the battle at the entrance to the goblin mountain.

"Let's go see it," directed the king.

"I have a picture in my mind, if you will allow, sire."

"We follow your direction," responded the king. Herman, Falslevia and the king became a streak of golden light above the trees.

The king got an immediate idea as he saw the mountain entrance. "Do we want them to know of the brilliance of the dust before they even come out of the mountain?"

"If I may speak, sire," said Falslevia quietly. She continued as the king nodded. "The cave is very dark inside. I have studied it. They have to be used to darkness, or very dim light."

"It's true, sire," joined Needles. "They stay away from the entrance, well back into the cave. They don't like the light." Needles saw the wonder in the king's eyes. "We hid in the brush in front of the cave and made ourselves very dim."

"We were well hidden," added Falslevia. The king was amazed at the courage of his faeries.

"I think that a blast of faerie dust would be good," remarked Herman. "But we should wait until they start to come out so they don't have time to talk about it and make additional plans. Our battle must be based on surprise." Herman then directed ten of the faeries, including Falslevia and Needles to prepare for a burst of brilliance.

"Now we wait until they decide to come out," said Herman quietly. "I hope all is ready along the trail."

"Your pals and my people will be ready."

CHAPTER TWENTY-TWO

THE BATTLE OF THE MOUNTAIN FOREST

"Forward, to the forest of the cowards!" screamed the king. The goblin hoard moved toward the entrance, one great mass of stinking flesh, moving on short stubby legs, and carrying a club in each hand, swinging them dangerously in the air. Ready or not, the war the faeries had feared was about to come upon them.

The fire drink had kept the goblins drunk and angry during the day. The goblin army moved out of their secure home to follow their king into battle.

"I like the dark," growled Shulkgak.

"Good," replied the king to Shulkgak. "We fight better when the cursed sun has gone away."

"Quiet, so's them cursed cowards can't hear us comin', until it's too late," said Gackix.

"Good idea," agreed the king. "Pass the word. Everyone to be silent. No sounds."

The goblin hoard moved on as a quiet shadow, blackening the ground as they passed.

"When we takes them by surprise, they's gonna fall like puny rocks under our clubs!" said the king as the goblin army passed in the shadows of the night, on the path that they hoped would ultimately lead them to the borders of the great forest kingdom of the faerie people.

Herman waited far from the trail coming from the entrance of the mountain so his glow would not be seen. He watched to see how large the army was. He was amazed at its great size. "We'd better be good," he thought to himself. He had sent all the others ahead. When the last of the army had left the entrance, he rose high into the air. A faerie was waiting for him in the air above the path, and suddenly flared with brilliance.

Falslevia had been watching for the signal. She flew to the others and the ten prepared to give the brilliant blast to the head of the goblin army. They kept themselves as dim as they could, hidden in the underbrush. As the army approached, the ten brave faeries suddenly appeared a little above the front ranks of the army. The goblin king and his companions saw them and cursed.

"What is that?" was the only thing they had time to say before their eyes were met with a brilliance that they had never experienced before. The flash of the dust only lasted a split second. The faeries then shot high into the vault of the night sky. The others waiting along the trail, seeing the flash, knew that the army was now coming, and made themselves ready for what was to come.

The goblin king and the first five ranks of the army were temporarily blinded by the brilliance. Their front rank comrades protected the rest of the army. Those that had seen the brilliance began swinging their clubs in fear, bashing the heads and bodies of their fellow army members. The king didn't know what had happened, but he knew that he must bring the army under control. In his terrible language, he yelled orders to his goblin hoard. Shulkgak understood what needed to be done and joined the king. They finally got the goblins calmed down. Their eyesight slowly returned, but they couldn't see as well as before.

"What was that?" asked one near the king.

"Don't know?" growled the king. "Some cowardly trick. You know now how they is cowards!" yelled the king at his army. "They will not come out and fight us. They uses tricks on us instead." He tried to appear sure of himself, but he was inwardly worried what other device the enemy might try.

"How we gonna protect ourselves?" asked Shulkgak.

"We is goblins! Does we fear these little puny cowards? We's gonna have their forest and their treasures!" yelled the king at his army.

The army gathered courage and began to march forward again.

As the army left the area, Herman dropped to the ground to inspect the damage that had been done. It was not a pretty sight. The goblins in their fear and panic had swung clubs effectively against their own comrades. Herman counted at least fifty either unconscious or dead; he couldn't tell which in the dim light of his glow. Then he got an idea. The clubs were laying all around. He wished his scout faerie would come so he could get the message to the ambushers. As he thought, Needles was suddenly beside him.

"Wow! They did that to themselves? What do we do now?"

"Go with all safe speed to the third ambush area, the steep part of the trail where we have the rocks waiting. Get fifty faeries to come back here with you. Get some from the next ambush area if you have to. I will be up above the forest so you can see me for a picture. Move as fast as you can."

Needles streaked away.

Falslevia waited on the trail. She heard the goblins approaching. Moussey and the other pals waited with the faeries at the first narrow ambush area. Suddenly a silver gold streak came down the path, dangerously fast.

"They are coming," whispered Falslevia. No one was quite sure how successful this would be. The ten faeries that had given the first flare of the dust had brought a report of the panic of the goblins.

"They will be ready this time," Moussey had told his little army. "They may be blinded, but they won't panic."

As the goblins approached the narrow part of the trail the king immediately saw the possibility of an ambush.

"Maybe we be attacked here," warned the king to the ones behind him. "Pass the word."

The ambushers heard the king speak, but didn't know what he said. When the goblins were within the narrow path ten faeries appeared in the air and their brilliance flared. As they appeared, the king covered his eyes; many of his army didn't. The pals only waited a few seconds, but it seemed like an eternity. The goblins waited, not swinging in panic. Goossey grabbed a club from a goblin that he could tell had been blinded. He hit the goblin hard and also the one next to him. The second one began swinging, taking down four of his fellow goblins. The same thing happened in two other places as the pals began their work of confusion. Faeries hovered above; dust fell and others lifted the clubs into the air. The king saw all of this and started yelling orders to his goblins. Some could see and others could not.

The clubs that the faeries had taken were suspended overhead. The goblins were watching this with fear and wonder.

Suddenly Falslevia darted in among the goblins, around their heads and legs. Other faeries caught on to what she was doing. The goblins must be put off guard; the faeries could not fight them hand to hand. The goblins began swinging at the streaks of light. At this moment of distraction, the faeries let the clubs fall. The faerie army hoped that the dust would not stick on the clubs when they fell. Some clubs fell fast enough to knock out a goblin, if it hit him, and some descended slowly back to the hoard and were picked up by the goblins. With the confusion Falslevia and her comrades were causing, the pals sneaked in and started bashing goblins, then retreating, then returning to bash. They discovered they had to hit the goblins hard in the head; this was no game. The goblins must be out of the action. The pals knew that this ambush had not been as effective as it needed to be; very few of the goblins were being put out of commission.

All these things were happening in the twinkling of an eye, and at the same time. Suddenly the battle took a turn in favor of the faeries.

The goblins that had picked up the clubs with the faerie dust on them started to scream in pain. The faerie dust was burning their hands. This caused major fear and panic. Falslevia and her brave comrades continued to dart in and out, and the pals moved in to bash heads. Then the inevitable happened. One of the goblins swung at the right time and hit one of the darting faeries. The young faerie was knocked out of the battle and hit a tree with such force that he was almost smashed flat. Suddenly all the faeries stopped.

Three more faeries were struck down as the goblins became aware of their presence.

"Get above the goblins," Goossey yelled. *"Now!"* The force of his command shook the faeries to action. They moved above the army. At the same time, the goblin king commanded the army to move forward. The faeries did not know what to do. Moussey moved to the side of a faerie and told her to pass the word. "Move to the rocks. We must be ready for them there. Tell everyone to rise high in the sky and move to the rocks."

As the end of the army passed, Herman dropped onto the path beside his pals. Some faeries were hovering where their comrades had fallen. "Come with me," Herman said to his pals. He flew to the one group of faeries who were looking in disbelief at the first faerie that had been struck and killed by the goblins. It was not a pretty sight. "There is no way to express proper grief or understanding," he gently said to the faeries, "but we must go on. We cannot let this stop us, or the goblins will enter the home forest and kill even more. Leave one faerie here," Herman pointed to one of the faeries, "and one of you go to the king in the meadow and send some here to take our fallen comrades back home." He indicated another faerie to be the messenger. "The rest of you," now he spoke with firm authority, "use your dust to pick up the clubs of the fallen goblins before they wake up, and come with me to the open area of the trail just before the steep section with the rocks. We will drop the clubs from there. While you have been fighting this battle, I have been testing the dust on the clubs. If they are dropped from a sufficient height, the dust falls off, then they can fall fast enough to do damage." He called to the other groups of faeries around the other fallen comrades. "We must move now, or we will lose the advantage of the clear area of the trail."

The faeries suppressed their grief into determination and began dusting the clubs, picked them up and followed Herman into the sky. There they were surprised to meet many more who were waiting with clubs from the first encounter with the goblins. "We have about one hundred fifty clubs," said Herman to his pals as they rose into the night sky. "Fear is our best weapon."

"Fear and confusion," added Moussey. "They are lost without their leader. If he can be stopped, they will have no direction."

Each of the pals carried two clubs. "You know Herman," said Cheesey, "it is a very new experience to hit someone as hard as we are hitting the goblins. We are larger than they are. I know they must be dead."

"We thought this would be an adventure," answered Herman, trying to console his pal. "But it is a serious fight for the life and rights of the faeries. The goblins have no right to take the faerie forest from the faeries. You know that they would kill many, if not all of the faeries in order to loot their kingdom."

"There they are," cried one of the faeries.

"Wait until I give the signal. The faerie next to me will flare his brilliance, then drop the clubs. Pass it on." The message passed quickly through the group.

When the tiny army in the sky was directly over the goblins, Herman gave the command and the faerie next to him rose a little higher and flared. The clubs dropped. "As soon as you drop your clubs, get to the rocks," Herman instructed his pals. "I have to get to the king and Ewanille. If we can put the goblin leader out of commission, Ewanille will be the final weapon."

"You hope," said Moussey, not completely convinced.

"You hope too," said Herman as he dropped his clubs and flew off to find the king and Ewanille to set up his next attack.

As soon as the pals dropped their clubs, they flew quickly to the rocks.

As the clubs fell and began striking the goblins, fear and chaos reigned again among them. When a club hit a target, which all of them didn't, the goblin fell, never to move again. Many of the goblins ran off the trail into the underbrush. Several around the king fell. He turned and saw many of his army running into the underbrush. He immediately ran back through his army to stop the chaos. As he yelled at his goblins, they calmed down and remained ready to battle. He could not get to the ones that had already left the trail. Clubs were falling on his fellow goblins and some fell close to him, doing no damage, except to frighten the goblins. After he got his army calmed, he looked up to the sky, from where the clubs had fallen. There he saw the power of these little people. "I didn't know they flew," he said, very discouraged. "Maybe better we waited for the scouts." He looked at the clubs; some still had a light glow on them. He picked one up. It was warm, and then hot to the touch. He dropped it. "What power they got?" he asked himself, out loud.

A goblin next to him spoke. "Gagluk and Kulshig was burned bad by clubs. Gold stuff burns."

The king noted that one third of his army was either out of commission or absent. "How these little, nasty things do this to my great army?" he thought to himself. "Keep lookin' at the sky!" he yelled at his remaining army members. "If you sees clubs fallin', move, and don't touch! They burns us." He walked back to the head of the army, encouraging his goblins as he passed them. Then he stood on a rock by the side of the trail and looked over the remains of his army. "We is goblins. Nobody beats us." The goblins started to take courage again. "These little scabs can't stop us. We gonna git their treasure and kill 'em for what they do to us. They is cowards. They fights in the dark from the sky. We knows they can't beat us face to face. Now let's go git 'em!"

The roar of courage from the goblin army could be heard throughout the mountains. Big people miles away would wonder for years what kind of weather could cause the wind to roar like that.

The goblin king gave the command to resume the march unaware of the surprises set by Herman and his tiny army.

Herman had flown on to find the king and Ewanille. The three remaining pals went to the place where the rocks had been placed. Falslevia, Shellane, and Andron were among the fifty faeries waiting for them. "How are things going?" asked Andron anxiously. "We have been waiting here all through the battles. We heard that roar. What was it? Is everything all right?"

"The roar was the goblins being courageous. But they have lost many and many have deserted into the woods," responded Goossey.

"The ambushes in the narrow places don't work very well. The goblins are too strong and big," added Moussey, "and I think they are now wise to the dropping of the clubs."

"We have lost four faeries," said Falslevia. "It was my fault. I shouldn't have started flying among the goblins."

"What you did was brave and necessary. It confused the goblins and allowed us to get some blows in among them that we wouldn't have been able to do otherwise," consoled Cheesey. "The ambush was not working. Something had to be done."

"We lost four of our number?" asked Shellane in disbelief.

"Yes," answered Moussey. "The king has been sought to bring them home to your forest. It's a terrible thing."

"But we really expected it," said Andron. "We just didn't want to say it out loud. But we all feared it. I am just surprised it has only been four. You were not wrong Falslevia. You did the right thing. We are here to fight for our forest. That's what you did."

"How will we know they are coming?" asked Moussey suddenly aware that the goblins might be near.

"We have scouts down the trail," said Shellane in response. "We will have plenty of time to prepare."

Suddenly Needles streaked into the group. "Isn't that a little foolish to move so fast in the forest," scolded Falslevia.

"Moving fast is what I do," responded Needles proudly. "The army is still far away. It is moving with caution. They don't know where the next ambush will happen."

"Too bad we can't harass them some more before they get here," Goossey thought out loud.

"Hey! I've got a great idea," exclaimed Cheesey suddenly. "What would happen to the goblins if you dropped some dust on them directly? Would it cause them to rise? They are scared of our flying. If they rose into the air a little, it would scare them to death."

"Then we could push them around as we wanted," cried Needles excitedly.

"What makes you think they will just sit there and let us do what we want to them?" asked Andron doubtfully.

"It took us a while to learn to fly," responded Cheesey with enthusiasm. "The goblins will not have you to instruct them. They will just be floating in fear."

Andron could feel the enthusiasm of the fifty faeries around him. He wondered if he should check with Herman or the king. Then he thought, "I am the faerie leader. I can make decisions."

"How will we accomplish it?" he asked cautiously. "How will we get the dust on them?"

Everyone thought a moment. "We could descend in large groups to a point just above them and outside of the range of their clubs, dust them and watch and wait," said a faerie named Joreena.

"We must watch out for their leader," cautioned Moussey. "He is less fearful than the rest of his army."

"Let's start at the back of the army," exclaimed Falslevia. Andron gave the signal and the faeries rose high into the sky, flying to the rear of the army before they descended. As they dropped to the army, fear appeared in the eyes of the goblins.

"Now what," one asked another. "What they goin' do now?" A few of the goblins mustered the courage to swing at the faeries, but stopped as they realized they were out of range. Suddenly the faeries turned over on their backs and their wings moved and the dust fell. The faeries and pals had forgotten one thing. The dust burned the goblins. The dust had always been their most effective and terrible weapon. The goblins had no defense against it. It immediately started to burn them. Some began to rise into the air. The chaos that followed was a fearful sight to see. The goblins that the dust had touched were writhing in pain; some were rising into the air, and others were running off the trail to avoid the terrible burning dust. The ones in the air dropped their clubs and roared in pain and fear and anger. The faeries bravely moved to push them around in the air. The goblins didn't move easily, but they did move. The faeries found that they were so afraid when they began to move that they stopped swinging; it was like they were frozen with fear. The faeries pushed and pulled them back toward their mountain.

Only about fifty of the goblins had received enough dust to rise into the air. But the chaos on the ground was very effective. The rear of the army was running in fear back toward their mountain; some were floating back toward the mountain, frozen with fear in the air. The dust did not last long on the air born goblins. They suddenly started to fall to the ground. When they hit, they immediately got up and joined the retreat to their mountain.

The goblin king could not tell what was going on. He sent one near him to find out what was happening. When he returned to the king, he could hardly speak. The king saw the terrible fear in his eyes. "Speak. Now!" roared the king. The goblin was jarred out of his trance.

"Some of 'em is floatin' in the air!" he cried. "Many is in pain, burnin'. Them cursed things dropped some stuff on 'em and they is floating an burnin'. Many is runnin' back home. These rats is terrible to fight. They has powers we can't fight."

The king was discouraged, but anger overpowered his discouragement. "The ones that runs back don't get treasure. We gits it all." He looked over the remains of his army. Over half of it was gone. "They is afraid of us in front. They knows we is the bravest. They leaves us alone. Let's get 'em and break 'em in their cursed forest!"

The army believed their king; they had not seen what the messenger had seen. The king saw the fear in the eyes of the messenger. "You come now or I kills where you stands," growled the king. The messenger moved on with the army. The king did not know what awaited him. If he had known, he would have given up the quest for the faerie treasures and returned to the safety of his mountain.

The pals and the faeries returned to the rocks to prepare for the next battle, pleased with their accomplishments, encouraged to continue the next stage of the war. It was three hours before dawn when the goblin king led his diminished army toward the steepest place on the trail. This part of the trail was narrow, and the tree cover was very thick; even the goblins' eyes had some difficulty in making out every detail of the trail. The goblin king expected another ambush in this narrow area. The trail turned suddenly and then went straight and up. The goblins proceeded warily and slowly up the trail. The king knew that the large meadow was at the top of this steep incline. He had been here often as he spied on the faerie forest. About a hundred feet from the top, the goblin hoard heard a rumbling sound; they stopped and tried to penetrate the darkness ahead. Suddenly a huge boulder appeared out of the darkness. The king barely had time to jump out of the way into the tangled underbrush along the trail. The boulder rolled its destruction through the army, crushing and scattering the goblins. Then there was silence, except for the groaning of the injured. The king slowly came back onto the trail and began to walk back through his army as the rumbling began again. Another boulder appeared out of the darkness. The king was caught in the middle of the main mass of his army. The army panicked this time. The goblins tried to get off the trail but merely succeeded in stumbling into each other, knocking each other down. The goblin king was in the middle of this panic. He pushed hard on his comrades, trying to move them away from him. He turned to see where the boulder was just as it crushed him and several members of his army as it rolled on its path of destruction. Another boulder immediately followed; the goblins had no time to regroup or move out of the way. They were tripping over the bodies of their dead and injured comrades. This third boulder veered off into the underbrush before it could do the total damage the faeries had expected.

Shulkgak had successfully avoided the first boulder by jumping into the underbrush. He had stayed there when the king started his investigation of the damage. He was in the protection of the underbrush when the second and third boulders came down the trail. He could not see the terrible havoc that the boulders were causing among his comrades. After the third boulder, silence again reigned, except for the cries of pain and anguish of the goblin army. Shulkgak rose from his place of security and began to move through the army. When he saw the king and those around him that had been crushed by the second boulder a grin curled his ugly lip as he realized the kingship could fall to him if he acted quickly. He began to yell at the remaining army members. "The king is dead! They has crushed him with their cowardly rocks. Is we goin' to let them git away with this? *We is the power in these mountains! We gots to git even!"*

Faeries had been stationed in the underbrush, hidden far off the trail. They had been appalled by the terrible effectiveness of the boulder attack. They had almost been run down by panicked goblins thrashing through the forest. These scouts were even more amazed that the goblins seemed to be listening to this new leader. Shulkgak wandered among the goblins, mustering them to further attack. "These cowards gots to be taught a lesson! We can't let 'em do this! We is stronger and bigger! We gots to git their treasure and take it to our mountain." As Shulkgak saw his success, another idea came to him. "And where is our scouts? They went to the forest of the cowards! They has not returned. They has been murdered by these cowards! *We gots to finish 'em off!"*

CHAPTER TWENTY-THREE

AFTER THE BATTLE

A rumbling sound warned the goblins that another boulder was on its way. *"Off the trail!"* yelled Shulkgak. The goblins immediately responded to their new leader. The boulder went straight down the trail, finishing any injured goblins that were unable to get out of the way. "How many more does they have?" asked Shulkgak to a goblin next to him. The goblins waited in fear for half an hour. *"Let's go git 'em!"* yelled Shulkgak. *"They gots no more cursed boulders!"* The scout faeries were again amazed that the army came out of the underbrush, gathered on the trail, and began marching upward.

One of the scouts immediately flew to the meadow where the faerie army was gathered and sought out the king and Herman. "They have a new leader and are still coming. He somehow talked them into continuing the fight."

"I have never seen such hatred!" exclaimed Herman. "But then I am not that old." The group chuckled quietly.

"We must use our last resort," suggested the king.

"You're right, Your Majesty," agreed Herman. "When all of the goblins are in the meadow, Ewanille will flare."

"When she flares, we must all cover our eyes. She is too bright for even our eyes. We have a blind faerie back in the kingdom that can testify to this. It is because of him that we know the extreme brilliance she can produce."

"Herman began to organize this final assault. "Pass the word. All the army is to move to the opposite side of the meadow, into the trees. The signal for Ewanille to flare will be my yell. We will wait until the whole army is in the meadow. After she flares, move in and drop the clubs we have gathered. We must produce as much chaos as possible."

The goblins moved warily up the last few feet of the trail. They stopped at the entrance to the meadow. "I doesn't see any of them cowards," whispered Shulkgak to a goblin at his side. "Does you?"

"No."

Shulkgak courageously led his much-reduced army into the meadow. He had instructed them to spread out so they would not hurt each other as they had in previous attacks. As Herman saw this, he was pleased. "Now they will all be exposed to Ewanille."

A faerie waited high in a tree to inform Herman when all of the army was in the meadow. Herman was watching the sky. Suddenly a point of light appeared and disappeared. "That's the signal." Ewanille, high in the sky above the meadow also saw the blink of her faerie brother.

She slowly descended from the sky. The goblins could see her at first as a point of light coming from the sky. "Hold your ground!" yelled Shulkgak. Herman's plan was working perfectly. All the goblin eyes were riveted on her. "What cursed trick is this?" whispered a fellow goblin to Shulkgak. Suddenly Herman yelled. The faeries covered their eyes. In almost the same instant Ewanille flared. The goblins had never been subjected to such brilliance. The whole meadow became as daylight. It was like a small sun had suddenly appeared inside their heads. At least half of the remaining army was immediately blinded, never to see again. They were among the unfortunate ones in the front ranks. The rest would not regain their sight for several hours and then it would be severely limited. Ewanille had been instructed to count to six, and then stop, lest she do herself harm.

As the light disappeared, Shulkgak, who had been totally blinded, fell to his knees. He had never experienced such pain in his head and more directly, his eyes. "We is beaten. Beaten by these cowards."

"They is not cowards," muttered a goblin next to him, equally blind. "They has more power than we has ever knowed. If I gits back to the mountain, and I don't knows how I will, I is goin' to tell about these powers."

"We was fine in our mountain. How we ever let the king talk us into this?" groaned another next to them.

Suddenly clubs began falling from the sky. The goblins were unable to protect themselves. They merely fell on the ground and covered their heads as best they could.

Seeing this pitiful sight, Herman called off the attack. "We must get them home to their mountain," said the king quietly. "They must not be allowed to roam the forest."

"We can dust them enough to make them float, and then push them to their mountain and drop them at the entrance," suggested Shandra.

"It will take a lot of dust," responded Moussey.

"We have a whole army," added Falslevia.

"We must also search through the forest and find those that are lost and take them back also. It will take a lot of searching," complained Falslevia.

"But it must be done," said the king.

"We must also return their dead to their cave. We cannot leave them to pollute the trail," added Shellane.

"We have much to do," said the king. He turned to Andron who had recovered and returned to the battlefront. "Go to the forest and bring all the rest of the army. We will need a great deal of dust to move all of these goblins to their mountain home."

"Scouts must be placed to protect us as we work during the day," said Herman to the king. "Ewanille's flare may cause big people to investigate. They can find the goblins, but not your people."

The king agreed. The faeries then began the huge task of returning all of the goblins to their home. "We should locate the lost ones, but only move them at night," suggested Herman. "We don't want them directly seeing your people.

"But the dust burns them!" exclaimed Falslevia. "Aren't they beaten enough?"

"I've noticed my dust doesn't hurt them as much as the dust from the older faeries," explained Needles.

"Are there enough young ones to do the job, Your Majesty." Herman was concerned about the same thing happening that happened to Jorran, Orria, and Greena.

"Yes," sighed the king. "But we will have to send to the center of the kingdom for them. I had hoped they could be spared seeing the goblins."

"I can get there fast, sire," said Needles. "We all know the canopy of the forest now."

"Go with all the speed you are famous for, my young friend," responded the king.

Needles became a golden streak of light.

When the young faerie dusting army arrived, the goblins were thoroughly dusted, more than the previous time during the battle. They floated in horror into the air. They felt themselves being pushed. They were so frightened they did not even speak. They knew that their captors couldn't understand them anyway. It required three faeries to move a goblin through the air. A large component of dusting faeries went with each group of moving faeries. The goblins were redusted as they began to sink toward the ground. It took two redustings to get them to the entrance to their cave. There they were left to slowly drift to the ground.

It was hard to find the ones that had run into the forest during the battles. They were found hiding under bushes, behind trees, and just generally cowering from whatever had attacked them. When they saw the glowing faeries coming at them, some ran, some just rolled into a ball and trembled. When daylight came, the faeries ceased their grisly work of taking them home to their mountain. It was necessary for the faeries to remain on guard in trees or some other place of hiding until the night came. Then they would resume their cleanup work. Some of the goblins still had their clubs so the faeries waited patiently until each fell asleep and then dusted the goblin and took him to the mountain immediately. The faeries took care of this work in shifts, making sure they did not deplete their individual supply of dust.

The goblin scouts in the faerie forest were dealt with in a similar manner to their comrades of the battle. They were thoroughly dusted, felt themselves rise into the air and then were gently pushed toward their mountain. They were curious about the points of silver gold light that surrounded them as they passed through the air. They had a completely different outlook on the experience than those of their comrades that had been attacked by these gentle people. They thought they had the hardest job, going into the faerie forest itself. Once they felt the support of the dust, they lounged back and enjoyed the ride. The faeries could not help laughing out loud at the sight. The goblins later told their comrades that they had never heard such a pleasant sound as the tiny, light voices in laughter. However, their arrival at their mountain shocked them into the reality of the situation when they saw their dead comrades piled in front of the mountain home; the reality of the war quickly brought them out of their feeling of comfort with their captors. The faeries felt sorrow as they saw the change come into the eyes of these goblins. Rapture suddenly turned to horror, terror, and hatred.

One of the faeries remarked to her comrade. "I really thought they might like us under favorable circumstances. I guess it is not really possible."

It took four days for the faeries to find all the goblins and return them to their mountain. Andron and Shellane were in charge of this unpleasant work.

When the cleanup began, Herman and the pals remembered that they had been gone from their homes for four days. "We have to go and report to our parents," Herman told the king. "We have often gotten an extension of our camping trips. We just have to make them aware of what we are doing."

The king looked at Herman and asked. "Tell them what you are doing?"

"Well, not everything." The pals left with twenty-five faeries accompanying them as an honor guard. They flew directly home, reported to their parents, renewed their provisions and returned to the faerie forest. The whole process took about twenty-four hours.

Herman had Andron report to him immediately upon his return. Andron had set up his outpost at the edge of the faerie forest. When the job was finally done, he came to Herman with some very unpleasant news. "Come with me," he requested of the young general. "There is something you must see!"

Herman flew at Andron's side, along with the king and all of the faeries that had been with them from the beginning: Orria, Shandra, Jorran, Falslevia, Greena, young Needles, and Ewanille. Actually there were about one hundred faeries as well as the other pals that went with Herman and the king to the goblin mountain. Herman wondered that Andron had requested that they go in the daylight. "What you are going to see must be seen in total daylight in order to get the full scope of the problem."

As they arrived at the mountain, all were shocked and horrified at the scene. The faeries had piled the dead goblins in front of the entrance to the mountain, assuming the goblins would take care of their dead. Nothing had been done. Many of the faeries had to leave. The stench was more than they could endure. "What will we do?" asked the king of his young general. "This is terrible. It is unacceptable. It is not right. How can they do this?"

"Their king is among those piled there," responded Needles. "They have no leader. They are frightened."

"They don't have the same feeling for their people as we do, I guess," added Orria.

"*Burn it!*" exclaimed Goossey. His voice was almost as harsh as the people lying in this grisly pile of death. All present were shocked at the suggestion.

Moussey was separated from the group, inspecting the entrance to the mountain. "They are deep in their mountain. No one is anywhere near the entrance. They are not going to do anything."

"How do you know that?" asked Shandra.

"I don't see anyone," Moussey responded.

"They could be deep in the cave," added Greena.

"I guess we have to find out," said Herman. "Who will accompany me into the mountain to find out if they are near? We can't see far enough into the cavern without going in."

He saw the fear and disgust in the eyes of all the faeries. He looked at his pals. "It is up to us. We now get to earn our money."

"Please give us a full renewal of the dust," pleaded Goossey. "We are going to need all the light and support that we can get."

As Herman and his pals started slowly into the mountain, they were pleased to have four very brave faerie friends accompany them. One was perched on each of the pal's shoulders, Orria, Falslevia, Needles, and Ewanille. "You don't have to come with us," said Cheesey, hopefully.

"But we would love your company," encouraged Moussey.

"We want to come," responded Falslevia.

"Yes, we decided that we needed to know more about the goblins to protect ourselves in the future," added Ewanille. "Besides, you may need some light down there."

The eight comrades crept into the mountain, rounded a bend, and suddenly the light from the day was extinguished. The light from the faeries and the dust on the bodies of the pals illuminated the passageway. The cave was still quite large, wide and high. They could not see the ceiling. "How far do we have to go," asked Cheesey, his whisper echoing off the walls of the cave.

"I don't know," answered Herman. "Until we think it's far enough, I guess."

The group continued farther into the cavern. Suddenly they heard the running of feet on the rock floor of the cave, farther ahead, in the darkness. But as they rounded another bend in the cavern, they noticed a dim light coming up from the depths. "They don't live in total darkness," discovered Greena.

"I wonder what the source of light is?" commented Needles.

"I don't intend to find out," added Goossey. "I think we have gone far enough!"

"I can flare if I have to," said Ewanille.

"Only as a last resort," commanded Herman.

"I hope there were not any side streets that we missed," complained Moussey. "It might be tough getting out of here if we get lost."

"They are obviously not near the entrance," said Needles. "Let's get out of here."

"The stench is getting unbearable," complained Goossey.

Suddenly a club came flying out of the dim light ahead. An ugly voice said something in the hideous goblin language. The group stopped. "We are now invading their home," said Greena. "Can you blame them?"

The group heard a sudden shuffling of many feet. Then they saw some goblins come into the light. They were different from the ones they had been fighting, "They are the females!" cried Orria in a whisper. "There are young ones at their sides."

The group saw no males, only females and children. "These will fight for their young," warned Needles. "We better get out of here."

"The little ones are cute in an ugly sort of way," said Ewanille.

The goblins were spread shoulder to shoulder across the entire passage. "They are not going to let us pass," said Goossey.

"They had only one club," said Herman, trying to calm the others. "None of them has any now."

"If they attack us here, we are not going to come out in very good shape," warned Needles. "Our curiosity is about to get someone hurt, maybe worse!"

"I think they are just as curious," added Orria. "They don't seem to be afraid."

"Oh, they're afraid all right," corrected Herman. "But they are curious, and I don't think they know completely what happened outside."

"When they find out, they will not be so quiet," added Goossey, warningly.

"We have found out that the army is not coming out," said Ewanille. "Maybe we'd better leave before these mothers and children find out that their men lost the war and hundreds died!"

"You're right, Ewanille," said Herman. "We found out what we needed to know. Any male goblins left are not going to come this far. Let's go."

The comrades turned slowly and started back up the passage. The faeries, still sitting on the shoulders of the pals turned and looked back at the goblins. "They are following!" cried Orria. "What will we do?"

Ewanille flew to a point in front of the goblins and flared, just slightly. The goblins stopped suddenly. The mothers pushed the children behind them.

"Keep moving," commanded Herman. "Ewanille, keep them back."

The goblins started to advance again. "They are much more brave than their male counterparts," said Moussey with respect.

Ewanille flared again, more brightly. The mothers had to cover their eyes. "I don't want to hurt them!" cried Ewanille.

"These little ones will grow up to be large ones, and they must not then decide to come against you again. They will not be so ugly-cute then. *They will be trying to kill you and steal your forest!*" yelled Herman, bringing the group back to reality.

The goblins had stopped; the comrades moved as fast as they could out of the cave. When they rounded the last bend and saw the light of day, they ran as fast as they could. The faeries hung on to their shoulders so they wouldn't get thrown off.

The faeries waiting on the outside had very worried looks on their faces when the comrades emerged from the cavern. The light of the day was very bright at first. "No wonder they don't like the light," commented Moussey.

"What did you find?" asked the king. "Are they coming out?"

"We saw only mothers and children," said Needles, sadly. The king was astonished.

"We saw none of the army. The only ones with courage to make contact with us were the mothers and the children." The King was surprised at the sympathy in Orria's voice.

"I think we should retreat a little and see what they will do," advised Herman. "They may come to the entrance. Maybe they will want to do something about this grisly pile of death."

The group waited for about an hour. "I don't think they are coming," said Andron. "Let's get on with Goossey's suggestion."

"Wait, I see something coming!" cried Shellane.

All strained their eyes to see into the dimness of the entrance to the mountain. Gradually the goblin mothers appeared, looking with surprise on the pile of their dead. The faeries and pals were astounded at the lack of emotion they witnessed. "They don't seem to care!" exclaimed the king.

"Or they can't show it, or we don't know what it looks like in their expressions," added Shandra.

"They are going back into the cave," said Needles, totally surprised.

"Maybe they are going for help to take them into the cave," encouraged Ewanille.

"Where would they put them in there?" asked Cheesey. "All of these dead would only add to the stench. The stench of death can't be the same as what we smelled in that place."

"Let's give them one more day," said Herman. "Then if they haven't done anything, we'll have to carry out Goossey's plan."

"I'm not really proud of my plan, as you call it. But what choice do we have?"

"None," answered the king. "Let's go back to the forest and get something to eat, spend the night and come back and see what has happened. If it is the same, then we can do what has to be done."

"Look!" exclaimed Needles. "Someone is coming."

One lone goblin mother returned to the entrance to the mountain. She looked at the faeries gathered in the air, slowly bowed, turned, and quickly disappeared into the darkness of the mountain.

All followed the king's lead and slowly rose into the air. The king nodded to Andron; all watched him, and then suddenly there was nothing but a silver gold streak across the top of the trees, heading for the edge of the great faerie forest.

CHAPTER TWENTY-FOUR

A JOYOUS COUNCIL

When the group arrived at the camp of the faerie army, they found it deserted, except for one lone faerie, not dressed in the normal faerie clothing, but a beautiful long flowing robe, which scintillated with all the colors of the rainbow, and some that the pals had never seen. The king was somewhat bewildered. "Where is the army? No order was given to return to the center of the kingdom."

"Please follow me, sire. The queen awaits you in the Council Clearing," answered the faerie.

The faerie immediately rose into the air and flew slowly along the trail into the forest. The king looked at the group; Herman signaled for them to follow. "What is this Council Clearing?" Herman asked the king.

"It is a large clear area just inside this edge of the forest," responded the king. "We gathered there for a council the first time we found murdered faeries, and it's the place where the decision was made to look for someone to help us. It has been called the Council Clearing ever since."

As the group arrived outside the clearing, Herman and his pals beheld a scene seldom witnessed by the faeries, and never before by anyone but the inhabitants of the faerie kingdom. The group came to a halt at what the pals assumed was the entrance to the clearing, but a drape of some very light, transparent material blocked their entrance into the clearing. The king whispered to Herman. "Please wait here. The queen has been busy. I know now what she is doing. Other faeries will join you here, the rest of us must go into the clearing to prepare for your entrance."

The pals were completely flustered. "I think some kind of special council has been convened and we're not supposed to be here," whispered Goossey.

"No, the king said they had to prepare for our entrance," corrected Moussey.

The material draping the entrance to the clearing did not allow one to see clearly what was going on within. Cheesey reached out to touch the material, but it pulled away from his hand, He quickly pulled his hand back. "Now that is weird."

"Maybe we should just sit tight until we really know what is going on," suggested Herman. The other pals accepted his gentle reprimand and patiently waited.

They became aware of some dust falling from above them; looking to the source of the dust, they saw some faeries descending. The faeries were in four groups, each group carrying some clothing of such delicate beauty that the pals were rendered speechless. The faeries shimmered with dust that looked different; it wasn't as golden as they thought it should be. As the faeries came closer, the pals could make out the detail of the clothing. Each group of faeries carried a tunic, pair of pants, cut like the ones the faeries wore, only large enough for the pals, and a robe, and a pair of shoes designed the same as those the faeries wore, but large enough for the pals. The faeries were all male. Andron was their leader. With great respect in his voice, he said, "Please do us the pleasure of changing into these clothes that we have brought to you."

"We are too dirty to put on such beautiful things," complained Cheesey.

"We have anticipated that," said Andron. "Please follow us."

The pals followed the faeries off into the forest a short distance. They came to a glen, with a pool in the middle. "Please remove your soiled clothing and bath yourselves. We will dispose of the clothing."

The pals looked at each other, bewildered, but quickly shed their soiled battle clothing. Immediately sixteen faeries descended and with their hands clad in the heavy leaves, picked up the clothing and disappeared into the forest.

When the pals had bathed and dried themselves with towels of curious workmanship, produced by the other faeries that had temporarily joined Andron's group, Andron and his companions helped the pals dress in the sumptuous clothing they had brought. "I have never seen anything so beautiful," commented Goossey.

"I feel real uncomfortable," added Cheesey, but with a broad smile of joy on his face.

"Hey! What is going on?" gently commented Moussey. The pals became aware of a shimmering, transparent wall of dust that enveloped them. They shimmered in the dim light of the forest floor, as they had never seen themselves shimmer with the dust placed on them for flying. When the dust had been placed on them to fly, they simply glowed. They looked up to the source of the dust and saw a very large group of faeries producing it.

"We're not glowing, we're shimmering. This is weird, man," whispered Cheesey.

"Andron and his companions also shimmer," added Herman.

Again Andron spoke with respect in his voice. "Please accompany us to the Council Clearing."

"How come you're talking to us differently?" gently asked Herman. "I guess we don't understand."

Andron winked at the pals and then spoke in the same respectful way. "Just be patient, all will be clear in a moment."

The faeries slowly rose into the air and began to move to the entrance to the clearing, but as the pals thought of rising to follow, they shot almost to the bottom limbs of the trees. "What's going on?" asked Goossey, not so gently.

The faeries immediately returned. "I'm sorry, extremely sorry and embarrassed!" said Andron with great concern in his voice. "The dust that has been placed on you is a special kind, used only for solemn ceremonies among our people. It is far more powerful than the normal dust. I should have had you walk instead of fly to the clearing entrance. It will take you some time to get used to using it to fly. I suggest you control your flying thoughts as much as possible. Please accept my apology."

"No sweat, Andron," chirped Cheesey, "but why are you treating us in such a respectful manner? Aren't we still buddies?"

Andron smiled. "Yes, we are still buddies, but as the faerie general of our army, it is my responsibility to lead the honor guard accompanying you to the clearing. Let me explain as you walk to the clearing. We will fly at your sides. You have done a great service for us, saved our kingdom. We want to show our gratitude for this."

"We didn't do it alone," added Goossey.

"Yeah," chirped Moussey. "You guys didn't exactly sit in a corner and suck your thumbs."

The faeries looked at each other and wondered why they ever would want to sit in a corner and suck their thumbs. Andron continued. "Trust me. And remember, when you get excited, the dust responds, ceremonial dust or regular. Try and control your emotions or you'll rise into the air, and much faster than with the regular dust."

"Why didn't we use this dust for the battles?" asked Cheesey.

"It is very taxing to produce in large quantities. All of us can't make it, and it takes great concentration and we fear would tax the strength of those that can if they tried to produce it in great quantities."

The pals accepted Andron's explanation.

"Well, here we are," said Andron. He smiled as he changed to his respectful tone of voice. "Would you do us the honor of accompanying us into the Council Clearing?" Then he whispered, "And remember, control your emotions." The warm grin on his face helped the pals relax as the drape opened and they entered the clearing. Herman and his pals were not prepared, nor could Andron have prepared them, for what they saw in the clearing.

All of the trees and shrubs, and the grass on the floor of the forest were covered with the shimmering dust. As they walked they could see it move from around their feet. The trees overhead closed together creating a roof of thick, intertwined limbs. The faeries were sitting or standing all around them, on leaves, on the limbs of the tress, and on the beautiful deep green grass that covered the forest floor. The clearing was at its widest point at the entrance. It became narrower at the far end. Fewer faeries were gathered at the entrance than at the far end. As the pals walked toward the narrow end of the clearing, they noticed that the number of faeries gathered increased. They also noticed that the faeries gathered behind them as they passed. All the faeries shimmered with the beautiful dust, making it hard for the pals to distinguish what awaited them at the far end of the clearing; their eyes were not used to such a display of brilliance. "I can't see very well," complained Cheesey. "Everything is so bright. It's all like a blur."

"Your eyes should get used to it as you walk," comforted Andron at his side. "We have to get used to this brilliance when we see it too."

"Squint your eyes," counseled Herman. "It helps to get used to it."

"Why the shimmering dust?" inquired Goossey.

"It is used for special occasions," answered Andron.

"And everyone is dressed so fancy," commented Moussey. "I have never seen such beautiful clothes."

"All part of the occasion," responded Andron. "Be patient and all will be explained."

As they had been talking, they had approached closer to the narrow end of the clearing and they now could see much better. "It's the king and queen," whispered Moussey.

"On beautiful thrones," added Cheesey.

"And look at Shandra," whispered Herman. Shandra's robe had many wonderful jewels sewn into the fabric and her necklace was of pure gold with one large deep blue jewel suspended at her throat.

"And gathered around them are Orria, Falslevia, Needles, Ewanille, Jorran, Shellane, Greena, all of our other buddy faeries," added Moussey.

Andron had to put his hand over his mouth to cover his laugh at the words "Buddy Faeries."

"I have never heard of faeries being buddies to big people," he chuckled.

"Well, they are!" exclaimed Cheesey, rather loudly. All of the faeries around them giggled. The sound of so many of the little people laughing was like the tinkling of a hundred tiny bells. The pals looked around them and recognized many who had been with them in the battles, many who had risked their lives for their forest and their way of life.

"I have never been so happy, or just plain full of good feelings for anyone in my life!" exclaimed Moussey.

"I know how you feel," added the other three pals.

To their embarrassment, they all started to rise. "Control your thoughts!" commanded Herman.

"I don't think I can, and I'm not sure I want to!" exclaimed Moussey, continuing to rise slowly upward. Again the delightful giggling of the faeries.

The other three pals descended to the ground. When Moussey saw this he controlled himself and slowly settled beside them on the grassy carpet.

By now they were almost at the foot of the thrones. The thrones were placed very high for faeries, so they would be at the eye levels of the pals. Herman and his pals had seen the power of the king and queen displayed in their home forest, but here they also saw them dressed in their royal robes, with many beautiful jewels about their necks and sewn into the robes. As they looked about them, they noticed that all of the faeries had similar things about their necks and in their robes, but none so brilliant as the king and queen.

The king stood. Herman and the pals bowed low, without even being told; it just seemed the thing to do. Then to their great surprise, the king bowed to them. The king motioned for them to sit. As they sat down, they noticed that all of the faeries were now gathered at the foot of the throne. The trees and shrubs seemed on fire with the brilliance of the shimmering dust about them. The king spoke.

"No doubt, my young friends, you are surprised, even somewhat overcome by this show of faerie power. Our royal robes of court are only worn on special occasions. The use of the shimmering dust is only allowed by my command, or the queen's, if she knows the occasion should merit it. Any other time it is prohibited. It is too bright and hard to control."

"Can you all produce this kind of dust?" blurted Goossey, immediately quiet and very embarrassed.

"No," gently replied the king. "Only certain faeries are born with the ability to produce the dust. They are trained from their births to control the power, but when they use it, the results are quite beautiful, even to us."

The king continued. "You accepted a call to help us, without even knowing fully what the consequences might be. We are all grateful you did not suffer injury, or worse. If we had not stopped the enemy," he would not mention the word goblin on this solemn occasion, "they would have taken over our forest, and the center of the kingdom, which is our seat of power. From there they could have caused great damage to the world outside. We could not allow it to happen. They had to be stopped at all cost."

The pals noted that the faeries had suddenly become very quiet, the shimmering dulled just a little. "But we have prevailed, thanks to your courage and leadership. Our kingdom is intact, the enemy has been defeated, and we honor you for your devotion to us, strangers until just a few days ago, and devotion to your own world, for it would have suffered had we lost the forest."

The queen arose. "We must let you return to your homes soon, but before we do, we would like to bestow some tokens of our appreciation upon you, and then have a feast before we bid you farewell."

The queen waved her hands and several faeries stepped forward with four necklaces of intricate design and beauty. Four faeries carried each necklace, as they had been constructed of sufficient size to fit around the pals' necks. The four sets of faeries slowly rose to the level of the pals' heads and gently placed the necklaces around their necks. At this point, the faeries could no longer hold their excitement. They all cheered together and gathered around and on the pals, expressing their gratitude. Tears of joy streamed down the cheeks of the young pals as they rose into the air, carrying their joyous burden of clinging faeries to the top of the protective canopy above the clearing.

Suddenly they were joined by their dearest friends among the faeries, those that had been sitting at the feet of the king. The other faeries gave way and Orria, Ewanille, Falslevia, Needles, Jorran, Andron, Shandra, Greena, and Shellane gathered around the pals, hugging them and kissing them on their cheeks, a great compliment that no other "big person" had ever received from one of the "little people." The king and queen politely invited all to descend to the floor of the forest.

A great feast followed, with delicacies that the pals had never dreamed existed. *"You have some great cooks!"* exclaimed Cheesey. *"My mother should get this recipe."* The whole company of faeries erupted in uncontrollable laughter.

Night had fallen outside the clearing, but the shimmering dust made it light inside. "We must return home, Your Majesty," Herman said, with great respect and regret. "Should it be at night or during the day?"

"At night would be the best, I think," responded the king. "Then you could return to your homes in the daylight."

"What about the dust?" asked Goossey. "It will be just a bit obvious when we get home.

"The shimmering dust will eventually disappear, and its enhanced power with it," answered Shandra. "Would tonight be sufficient, father?"

"I believe Shandra is right," said the king. "Then we can replace it with normal dust for your flight home."

"There is still something else that must be checked," said Moussey, solemnly.

"True," added Andron. "We have to return to the mountain."

"You're right," said Herman, joining the conversation with his voice of command. "May I suggest, sire, that we check the mountain tomorrow morning, do what has to be done, if anything, and then fly home tomorrow night."

The king gave his approval.

Slowly the enthusiasm of the faeries was replaced by fatigue from the events of the previous days, and all fell asleep. Herman and his pals were not able to sleep for some time as they talked quietly into the night about all of the wonders they had witnessed and experienced as guests of these powerful, courageous, tiny people.

CHAPTER TWENTY-FIVE

THE PALS GO HOME

arly the next morning, after changing into everyday clothing, the pals, the king, and the close companions of the pals, returned to the entrance to the goblin mountain. The faeries had made exact duplicates of the clothing Herman and his pals had brought with them before the battle. The terrible pile of goblins had been removed, nothing left to mark the spot but a terrible yellow stain on the ground, left by the blood of the fallen goblins. "Look!" whispered Shellane.

Three goblin females and two males appeared at the entrance to the cavern. They surveyed the faeries suspended in the air, saw the pals suspended with the faeries, fear came into their eyes, but they slowly bowed to the faeries, said something in their hideous language, turned and retreated into the darkness of the goblin mountain.

"That is weird," said Moussey quietly.

"It is—weird you call it?" asked Greena. Herman nodded his head.

"Yes, weird is the word," added Shellane.

"I think they were thanking us," said Ewanille.

"Thanking us!" exclaimed Orria.

"Yes. We had returned their dead so they could take care of them."

"You know I think you are right, Ewanille," added Herman. "That sound in their language may have been a thank you."

The king slowly rose into the air above the mountain entrance and the group followed. "Let's go back to the forest and move the army home to the center of the kingdom."

As the group arrived at the edge of the forest, Herman took the king aside from the group. "I think you should always place guards here at the edge of the forest, and at the entrance to the mountain. You must always know what the goblins are doing."

The king shuddered at the thought of placing any of his people near the entrance to the mountain, but knew that Herman was right.

"It will be done, my young general," the king said with a smile.

It took the remainder of the day to move the army back to the center of the forest. Moussey had never seen the center of the forest, so all the pals went back to spend the day with the faeries in the center of their kingdom. The king informed Herman and his pals that they would be welcome any time in the faerie kingdom. Faeries would always be watching at the pals' forest.

A scout dropped from the canopy of the forest and informed all that the sun had set. Final goodbyes were said, and Herman and his pals rose to the top of the forest canopy, and accompanied by their dear friends as an honor guard, became a silver gold streak, splitting the western sky as they returned to their homes with the speed and protection of the marvelous dust of power.

EPILOGUE

Herman and his pals left the kingdom with their honor guard, nine of their new-found, very dear friends from the faerie kingdom, namely: Falslevia, Greena, Orria, Needles, Shellane, Shandra, Jorran, Andron, and Ewanille.

Since the boys had been gone for quite a while, there really was not time to do much visiting with their comrades. They really had to get home so they could report back to their parents.

Cheesey asked, "Where are we going? We can't just fly to our homes."

Andron responded to Cheesey's question. "The best place for us to take you, because we'll all be glowing, is to the glade in your home forest where we first revealed ourselves to you."

"That's a good deal," said Moussey. "We can pick up the balls that we lost from our games of 500. We'll take them home with us and our parents will think we are amazing to have found them all."

The rest of the trip was uneventful and as they arrived at the glade in the pals' home forest, and slowly descended to the beautiful grassy carpet.

Moussey remarked, "This makes me homesick for your kingdom. This grass is throughout your kingdom, and although your kingdom is somewhat small for us, the beauty of the trees, and grass, and flowers was very hard to leave behind."

"Yes," added Herman. "Seeing that reproduced here, even in miniature, makes us home sick, even though we are coming to our own homes."

"How long will it take," Cheesey asked, "for the glow of this dust to disappear?"

"We don't know," responded Shandra. "We never timed how long it took you to get rid of it."

"We gave you a new supply half way over the ocean," said Orria.

"And that has lasted you this far," added Greena.

"So we really don't have the slightest idea," continued Shandra, "how long this most recent renewal of the dust will last."

However, Andron did notice, "You are not as bright as we are. When we first dusted you, you were. So the dust is already wearing off."

"That's true," added Ewanille, "But will it fade more slowly or more quickly, now that you are not under stress of battle?"

Moussey answered her question. "Oh yes. Under stress, thinking of flying, thinking of going fast, or moving quickly from one place to another causes it to be used up more quickly than if we're just in straight flight or just sitting around."

"Well," said Greena, "You're not doing anything now but just sitting around."

"I guess that's why the king told us to come home in the dark. He knew we'd have time to just sit, talk to you and let our dust fade."

"Okay," said Cheesey, changing the subject to reality. "Who's going to be the scouts to watch the edge of this forest? You're going to have to watch more than just during the summer. There's winter, spring…

"Yeah," added Goossey. "Who's going to be there? How will we know how to find you?"

"That's a good question," Jorran responded. "That's a good question. We have never really thought about it."

"We never really discussed it with the king," added Andron.

"Well, I think two of us should stay to start with," said Shandra.

"Yes but its sure going to be boring," said Moussey, "because we're not going to be there all the time."

"Moussey's right," said Herman. "We have to go home and sleep, 'cause our parents will not let us camp forever."

"I don't know," said Cheesey. "Maybe our parents would let us do that."

"You know they won't let us do that," Herman said. "We've got things to do around the house. I mean our parents are really good with us to let us go out, but once in a while they want us there to mow the lawns, weed the gardens, and they go on some trips and stuff, and we like to go on trips with them."

"Why couldn't the scouts go along with you on your trips?" asked Greena.

"Go along with us on our trips!" exclaimed Herman. "How could you do that?"

"Well, ride in your pockets," said Shandra with a mischievous grin.

"Ride in our pockets," said Moussey. "We don't all go together when we travel."

"That's right," Herman told the faeries. "Our family goes one place, Cheesey's goes another and so on."

"We'll just pick who we want to go with," said Andron.

"You're really serious about this, aren't you?" remarked Goossey.

"Sure we are," said Orria. "Here's a chance to get acquainted with your families."

"Yeah, but it sounds to me like you're planning on staying here quite a while," said Goossey.

"Well, if we ever have any other problems," said Jorran thoughtfully, "are they only going to happen in the summer?"

"Yes, what if they happen in the winter?" asked Needles.

"What about the winter. What happens in the winter in your kingdom?" asked Cheesey.

"In the winter it snows," answered Shellane.

"It snows in your kingdom?" asked Moussey, somewhat surprised.

"Think about it," said Orria. "The trees are very tall and thick so they keep out light, but snowflakes fall through them."

"Don't they fall through your trees?" asked Ewanille.

"Yeah, but if you're underneath them there is not much gets to you," responded Moussey.

"Well there is not much comes into our kingdom either," said Shandra.

"But there is a little bit that filters through the trees, and it's a little bit cool, so we have to wear coats,' said Needles.

"Coats?" asked Goossey.

"Oh yes," said Andron. "It's cold. We live near the mountains."

"How would you expect it to stay warm?" asked Shandra.

"I guess we hadn't even thought about it," said Herman.

"You thought it was summer all the time in our kingdom?" asked Jorran.

"Well, I guess so," said Cheesey.

"No it's not," said Orria.

"There is one thing that doesn't happen," said Shellane, "that happens to your forest that doesn't happen to ours."

"And what is that?" asked Cheesey.

"Our trees don't shed their leaves."

"What!" exclaimed the pals together.

"Your trees don't shed their leaves," said Moussey, not able to believe what he had heard.

"No," said Needles. "They don't."

"It's part of the marvel of these trees. They've been used to the dust for so long that they…they don't shed their leaves," continued Orria.

"Your forest stays green clear through the winter?" marveled Herman.

"Yes," answered the faeries together.

"I know it's unbelievable to you, but these trees here do not shed their leaves in the winter," said Shellane.

"Ah, but there's no faerie dust," said Herman.

"You're right," said Andron. "There is not faerie dust unless we're here and we are not here all the time."

"So what happens," joined in Shandra, "is that the trees have grown under the power of the dust."

"And they just grow that way," added Greena.

"That's the beauty of it," added Needles.

"That is marvelous," remarked Herman.

"So you have a little snow on the grass in the kingdom?" asked Moussey, getting back to the original conversation.

"Yes. We have a little bit of snow that comes down through the trees," said Shandra.

"And once in a while," said Greena, "a great big bunch falls as the weight get too much as it collects high in the trees and the leaves give a little bit."

"We've had to strengthen our homes," added Ewanille. "Because when that falls in one big chunk, it's very heavy."

"We had a terrible accident. It's been many years," said Andron, "where a big bunch of snow fell and crushed one of the homes. It was a terrible thing."

"My word," said Cheesey. "A whole family?"

"Yes," said Jorran, sadly remembering.

"Oh, my goodness," said Goossey.

"You have many things to watch for," said Herman.

"So the dust doesn't put a force field around you, huh?" asked Cheesey.

"A what!" exclaimed the faeries together.

"A force field. A protective barrier," continued Cheesey.

"A...No," answered Orria. "It doesn't."

"Well, I guess it does to a certain extent. The trees are very thick and no light gets out. The dust does have a protective power," said Shellane.

"Yes," added Greena. "But things can still come in. The Goblins got into the forest. They didn't have a"...she looked at the other faeries with a smile, "force field? As you call it, to deal with."

"Gee," said Goossey. "I kind of thought when you said the power of the dust, that that's what it was, a power."

"It would be very nice to have it that way," said Ewanille, "but that's just not the way things work."

"That's why we were so frightened," said Shandra, "when we knew the goblins were going to come. We knew we couldn't keep them out."

"So what's this power that the king talked about?" asked Cheesey.

"The power of the center of the kingdom," said Shellane. "You want me to do this, Shandra?"

"Go ahead. Be my guest."

"The power of the center of the forest," continued Shellane, "is a concentration of all the faeries. All the faeries live there and they have lived there for hundreds of years. It's like the dust has affected everything to where there is almost a presence of something, that we can't explain, that emanates from the center of the kingdom. And the farther out…"

"Can I continue?" interrupted Shandra.

"Go ahead," said Shellane, smiling. He knew she wanted to anyway.

"Thank you," she said. "The farther from the center you get, the less you sense that presence of power, for the power of the kingdom has created a center place."

"What do you mean by center place?" asked Goossey. "If the power of the kingdom is from all the faeries being together, then no one could take your power unless they took it from all of you at once, no matter where you were."

"Well, sort of," said Greena. "But it's a little more complicated than that, actually a lot more complicated."

"We think," said Orria, "that it has something to do… and we really don't understand it; we just know that it's there. There is a presence of power at the center of the kingdom."

"It could be a combination of all the faeries together," continued Jorran. "It could be that the center has had the dust on it for so long that it just emanates that power."

"And it could be," Needles added, smiling cautiously at the other older faeries.

"Go ahead," said Shandra.

154

"Well I learned in school, yes we do go to school," as he noticed the surprise on the faces of the pals. "We have to learn about faerie lore, and the outside world – everything we know about it. We have flying lessons, tree lessons, plant lessons, gardening lessons…we grow gardens. You never got to see those did you?"

"Please continue, Needles," encouraged Shandra.

"Yes m'am. We've learned that we don't know whether the power is like Shellane and Shandra have said, an actual somewhere or some-place at the center of the kingdom from where the source of the power is, or whether it's because we're all there, or whether we've been there for so long that the center of the kingdom is actually a seat of power. But in the center of the kingdom, I don't know whether you noticed, all of us are equally bright."

"I didn't notice that," said Cheesey.

"Neither did I," added Goossey.

"But I did notice," said Moussey, "that outside of your kingdom the king and queen are more bright than the rest of you."

"Yes. They are," said Shandra. "It's something about the way the dust recognizes their position as king and queen."

"You mean," asked Cheesey, thoughtfully and almost afraid to ask it, "that the dust has a mind of its own?"

"No. It only reacts with us, or with you, or with the goblins," said Andron.

"It doesn't like hatred, or mean attitudes, and it doesn't like evil," said Orria. "But it does respond to intelligence."

"So has it been responding to intelligence for so long that it has an intelligence of its own?" asked Herman.

"No. But there is something to do with its relationship with us, over hundreds of years, that makes it one with us," said Ewanille. "So at the center of the kingdom its power is equal in all of us."

"And if anyone figured out," said Jorran, "how to control that power outside of the kingdom… well that's what we were afraid of with the goblins."

"We didn't know if they would learn to use that seat of power. We don't know whether other big people could learn how to use it," said Shandra.

"They can't get us," said Greena, "to do it for them."

"But if they could trap us, a big group of us, that combined power of the dust on all of us could be used in ways that might be dangerous," said Needles, looking for and receiving nods of approval from the other faeries. "Maybe. And it's that maybe that we learn in school so we are aware that there is great power in the dust."

"We don't know the full power of the dust," said Andron. "We don't know if it is intelligent, and we don't understand how it interacts with us. We just know it does."

"And it seems to know if we want it to interact with something else," added Orria.

"And there are certain things it can't control," said Ewanille. "Like when it burned the goblins."

"But it didn't burn us," said Cheesey.

"I wonder if we had some really mean criminals," said Goossey thoughtfully, "if it would burn them."

"I don't know," said Greena. "But it wouldn't surprise me."

"But what you're saying is that if you want it to be on someone, it usually responds," said Moussey.

"But what if you became evil?" asked Cheesey.

"That's a problem," said Shandra. "The two rogue faeries that we talked rather impolitely about and the king disciplined us for it…"

"Yes, I remember that," said Herman.

"They were very unpleasant young faeries, two boys," Shandra continued. "But they are not boys anymore. It has been three or four years since they left the kingdom. They were still flying, so we assume that the dust is really a part of us, and when we live in a place for so long, the power of that dust permeates the trees, the grass, shrubs, flowers, the air, and it starts to build a presence of power. In other words, if we lived here long enough, there would be a center of power here."

"But we don't come here often enough and long enough," said Shellane.

"I see," said Goossey. "So those rogue faeries could be flying around the world someplace, making trouble."

"Well, it wouldn't surprise me," said Andron.

"They were always interested," said Orria, "in making contact with the big people. And that's what scares us. Remember that's the reason the king first came out of the forest, because he had been convinced to make contact with big people."

"I remember that story," said Goossey.

"Well, the king got wise, but those two rogues were very upset when the king went back into the forest," said Needles. "Yes, Shandra. That's part of our education."

"That's interesting," said Shandra thoughtfully, "I didn't know that had become part of your education in the schools."

"It almost has to be," said Ewanille. "I'm not that old and I remember hearing about that in school. They do it to warn us about improper use of our power. I think that the faerie elders think that those rogues keep their ability to fly."

"Which means," said Shellane, "they keep the power of the dust with them."

"It would not be anywhere near as concentrated." quickly joined Falslevia, who had been taking a nap and had just joined the conversation. "It's not as powerful as it is on us because we're at the center of the kingdom more, so it couldn't be as powerful on them."

"Will it eventually disappear and die on them?" asked Cheesey.

"We don't know that," said Shandra.

"And we don't want to find out," said Shellane.

"But we have to assume," said Falslevia, "that if we stay away from the kingdom long enough, the power of the dust would diminish. But we don't know for sure."

"It's also possible," said Jorran, correcting Falslevia, "That we might create a power of our own."

"That's right," said Shandra, "We just don't know the answer to all these questions."

"It seems to me," said Moussey, "there is a good possibility that those two rogue faeries are out in the world causing trouble."

"We hope they just got lost," said Orria, hopefully.

"But you really don't believe that do you?" asked Herman.

The faeries looked at each other and said together, "No."

"We really don't believe they are lost. We believe they left the forest," said Shandra.

"The king doesn't like us to say that," added Andron. "He wants to believe that they are lost or even dead."

"It's not a very nice thought to think they are dead," said Greena. "But the thought of those two out in the world, making alliances with big people…"

"That is scary," said Moussey. "There are big people out there that would make terrible alliances."

"They will take advantage of such a situation. It would be very bad," added Cheesey.

"You're right. It could be very dangerous," said Shellane.

"Well, we've established that the dust is quite powerful, I guess," said Moussey.

Everyone looked at him in disbelief. "Yes, I guess we have," said Greena, smiling.

"Well, the sun's coming up," said Shandra. "We'll walk you through the forest to the outer edge. Then we'll all go home and see what the king wants to do."

"So then who's going to stay?" asked Cheesey.

Orria raised her hand. "I'll stay."

"I'll stay," said Needles.

"Okay. You two stay," said Andron.

As the sun rose, its light gently filtered down through the leaves of the forest. The group walked quietly to the edge of the forest. No one spoke. Their minds were full of memories of new friends, comrades in arms, and the terrible experiences that they had suffered. Everyone seemed to be lost in their own thoughts. It really wasn't difficult as the faeries spread out through the forest to make sure they didn't miss any of the pink ribbons, as they didn't want them to lead anyone back to the glen. They had decided before leaving the glen to make sure all ribbons were found.

When they reached the edge of the forest Cheesy said," I hope we can remember the way back to the glen. We may want to go there sometimes just to relax."

"You have a point," said Greena. "This is quite a large forest. Not as large as our home forest, but still, it might be difficult to find your way in to the glen."

"Maybe we'll just have to have some picnics in the glen with you guys," said Goossey. "Then you can show us the way in, and if we do it often enough, we will learn the way."

"We just need to learn the land, bush, and tree marks that will lead us to it," said Herman.

"But we really don't want to make a trail into the glen," said Cheesey. "And remember there is no force field to protect it."

The faeries giggled. The pals always loved to hear that delightful sound.

As the comrades neared the edge of the forest, the sun became brighter, the trees less dense.

Just inside the edge of the forest Needles asked," How far do we get to follow?" He looked imploringly at Shandra.

"You have to stay inside the forest until we find out what the king wants to do," she said.

"Aw shucks," said Needles, disappointed.

"We probably should say goodbye right here then," said Greena. "I don't want to, but I guess we have to." The others nodded.

The pals did not know how to give such small, delicate creatures a hug, but the faeries showed them how. They lightly flew to their shoulders and gave them each a kiss on their cheeks. After giving the pals a kiss, each flew up into the lower limbs of the trees. The pals noticed that all the faeries gave them a kiss, the boys and the girls. They seemed to be waiting to say goodbye.

"Can you fly home in the daylight?" asked Moussey.

"Yes. We don't have to wait. The sun is brighter than the faerie dust," said Andron.

"No one sees us at all in the day time," added Orria. "It's a good time to travel"

"That's right," said Shellane. "But now you don't have to wait. You can go home in the morning, having lost most of the dust."

"Think rise," said Needles. "See if you can."

Moussey did it and did lift a little off the ground.

"Don't think rise," said Needles.

Everyone laughed. The departing faeries waved and disappeared into the canopy of the forest. Orria and Needles flew to Moussey's and Cheesey's shoulders.

"Where are you going to stay?" asked Herman.

They looked around and found a tree with thick leaves. "We'll be up in that tree," said Orria, pointing. "Think you can find it again?"

"I think so," said Goossey.

"If you come to the edge of the forest, we'll hear you and come to you," said Needles.

"Okay, but don't come if we have anyone with us," said Herman.

"Why would you have anyone with you?" asked Needles.

"We do have others that are our friends. We all play in the forest," answered Moussey.

"We'll just make sure we continue to stay at the edge of the forest," said Moussey.

As the pals walked out of the forest, they were four very excited boys. As a group they looked around them, and seeing no one, rose into the air and started toward their homes, about two miles away.

"Look at them," said Orria to Needles. "They're terrible. I want to go out there and scold them. But I guess we should let them have their fun."

"You're right, Orria. But they will use up the dust faster. That's probably what they are doing."

"I thought they would do it inside the edge of the forest," continued Orria.

"We really shouldn't be doing this," said Herman.

"No we shouldn't," said Cheesey.

"I agree with you," agreed Goossey.

"But we're going to do it anyway," said Moussey.

"We need to use up the dust," said Herman. "But we could end up a hundred feet in the air and suddenly have the dust go away."

"I guess we'd better drop back to the ground," said Cheesey.

"The dust is quite weak on us," said Moussey.

"I guess we're okay. Just don't think fly," directed Herman.

The four pals happily walked off together toward their homes. As they walked, they talked about the power of the dust.

"I wonder if the dust can be collected," said Cheesey, thoughtfully. "We could put it in a sack and keep under our bed, or something."

"Put it in a sack and store it under our beds?" asked Herman in disbelief.

"You know," said Moussey. "That just may be a possibility. We'll have to remember to ask the faeries about that next time we see them."

"So what would we use it for?" asked Herman. "If the faeries need us, they'll supply the dust. All we would have it for is to play, and that could be very dangerous and very wasteful of their dust"

"We also don't know," said Goossey, "How much dust it would take to fill a sack."

"Good point," said Cheesey. "How much dust to they actually put on us to get us to fly? Is it a sack full or a hand full?"

"Or two hands full," added Moussey.

"We don't know," said Goosseey.

"Right!" said Herman in his commanding general voice he had learned in the Goblin War. "That means we don't play with it!"

"Well what if those rogue faeries show up," said Cheesey.

"Yeah. What if those rogue faeries show up," added Moussey.

"And we need to do things by ourselves," joined in Goossey. "It would be nice if we knew how much dust they put on us so we could have our own supply."

"It sure would have helped, I have to admit," said Herman, "to have had our own supply during the war."

"I would have loved to have had it," said Moussey.

The others looked at him thoughtfully as they remembered how close he had come to the ultimate sacrifice.

"I guess it's worth considering," Herman admitted. "You guys are right. But I don't think we need it under our beds."

"Okay, Okay," exclaimed Cheesey. "I agree. But I think we need to have some type of extra supply if we ever work with the faeries again."

"Even if we go playing with them," said Goossey.

"If we go play with them we don't need and extra supply," said Moussey.

"Okay, Okay. We'll just stay away from them," said Cheesey.

"How are we going to stay away from them?" asked Moussey.

"Okay, Okay," said Herman. "Just let it go. But we do need to talk to the faeries about a dust supply. It's something to think about."

ABOUT THE AUTHOR

Jay Andrus grew up in a rural area of Utah where his friends and he spent all of their time outdoors inventing and playing their own fantasy adventure games in the fields and orchards surrounding their homes. Jay learned from his father to split kindling and haul coal to their three coal-burning stoves which heated their house, built before the turn of the 20th Century.

He now has his own wood-burning stove which heats their house in the winter. Jay thoroughly enjoys finding, sawing into the proper lengths, and then splitting the logs for their stove. He also enjoys helping his wife, who is an excellent quilter, pick out the colors for her quilts. She even asks his advice on the patterns of her quilts, sometimes.

Jay has always enjoyed music and singing and is a retired vocal/choral music professor. He has been telling adventure stories since he was twelve years old. He began with his nieces and nephews and continued with bedtime stories for his children and grandchildren, who seldom fell asleep until they had heard the last words of the story. This was never more evident than during their annual family camping trips in their tent in Capitol Reef National Park where his children anticipated a story each evening. They all know Herman and his pals and the faeries.

Fantasy Adventure is his favorite escape. Jay's favorite authors are Edgar Rice Burroughs, Anne McCaffrey, and J.R.R. Tolkien. Jay and his wife, Phyllis, are the proud parents of four daughters: Jaymie, Tamara, Kristen, and Tara (named after a princess of Mars). They have twenty-two grandchildren and six great-grandchildren, so far. They enjoy listening to classical music, watching good movies, traveling and doing family history.

CPSIA information can be obtained
at www.ICGtesting.com
Printed in the USA
BVHW030201160620
581641BV00001B/134

9 781634 174985